CW01500874

Spies by Moonlight

Kevin Doherty

First published in 2025 by Blossom Spring Publishing
Spies By Moonlight Copyright © 2025 Kevin Doherty
ISBN 978-1-917938-08-2
E: admin@blossomspringpublishing.com
W: www.blossomspringpublishing.com
All rights reserved under International Copyright Law.
Contents and/or cover may not be reproduced in whole
or in part without the express written consent of the publisher.
Names, characters, places and incidents are either products of the author's
imagination or are used fictitiously.

Also by Kevin Doherty

Patriots
Villa Normandie
Charlie's War
The Leonardo Gulag
Landscape of Shadows

For the grandchildren
Jemimah, Joseph, Leo, Stella, Caleb, Peter, Esther,
Miriam and Halvard

Acknowledgement

I am indebted to Hugh Verity's meticulous history of 161 Squadron, published as *We Landed by Moonlight* (Ian Allan Limited, 1978). Group Captain Verity flew many of the squadron's missions himself and was, perhaps, the most outstanding pilot of them all.

Prologue

Normandy, German-occupied France: May 1944

Marie Clément closed her eyes and tilted her face to the morning sun. She had lived all her nineteen years in this little white cottage, knew every stone in its walls, every beam and rafter. She let the sun's rays warm her for a few moments, her thoughts drifting across the years, then she hefted the copper basin of wet laundry against her hip and carried it down the yard to the clothes line. She wrung out the garments gently by hand – cotton dresses, blouses in white Chantilly lace, satin lingerie – their clean smell mingling with the scent that drifted from the lavender growing by the cottage door. All the garments were new and unblemished; nothing was patched or thinning or shabby. Heinrich told her that they came from Paris, from the very best couturiers.

'Nothing but the best for you, meine Liebe,' he would say. 'Try this dress for size. Let me look at you. Turn around. Ach, such beauty! Come here, let me hold you!'

He would take her in his arms and kiss her, teasing until he won a smile from her. Sometimes he would hum a tune and swing her into a waltz that swept them from room to room and out to the yard. They would end up laughing like children as they collapsed together on her bed.

She had so much to be thankful for. Heinrich – her Heini – did everything he could to bring her happiness. He was gentle and loving, and he looked after her with kindness. Nothing could release her from her sorrow over the loss of Maman and Papa, but in Heinrich's company she was able to set the sorrow aside for a time. And certainly she felt no guilt. Why should she feel guilt simply because her Heini was a German officer? It was not his fault that he and his comrades

1

had been sent to occupy her country. And occupation was surely better than outright war. Here in Belville, people understood that. No one in Belville would accuse her of collaboration. No, no one here in Belville.

That explosion last night. She had heard nothing, was sleeping soundly. Heinrich woke her to say he was leaving.

'Something's happened,' he explained. 'An explosion like that could be a serious matter. It sounded not far away.'

'But you said you're not on duty tonight.'

'I know, meine Liebe. A soldier's life, you see.'

One brief kiss, then he was gone.

She sighed. She was wasting time. She must get on with her tasks, like a proper German Hausfrau would. She had the cottage to tidy and this laundry to finish. And she wanted to take fresh flowers to the grave that Maman and Papa shared – they were at rest in the graveyard by the ruined church that stood right beside this cottage and its piece of pasture land that were her property now.

It was as she was raising the clothes line that she saw the man. She stepped back in alarm.

He was standing in the tall grass by the barn. How long had he been there? She did not recognise him; he was not from Belville. He was a stranger. An outsider. Outsiders, whether French or German, could bring danger, to her and to Heini.

He raised both hands, the palms towards her. Perhaps he was trying to indicate that he meant her no harm. He took a step forward – he seemed unsteady on his feet – then he spoke.

'Help me. Please.'

Part One
Full Moon

Tangmere, England

As operations went, that night's could have come straight from a textbook – had there been a textbook for what Archie Wyndham and the other Lysander pilots of 161 Squadron were doing. They had invented the whole thing from scratch, finding out what worked best as they went along, finding ways to do the impossible. And all of it shrouded in the deepest secrecy: even their fighter-pilot comrades were not let into the secret. 'Special Duties' was the anodyne title under which they served.

'That tells you all you need to know,' Archie would say to anyone with too many questions.

'It tells me nothing.'

'Quite.'

At 2245 hours, the moon was high in the sky over RAF Tangmere as Archie took off – the moon that governed his life, so that he no longer thought or calculated in terms of next week or this month but only in terms of this or that moon. A week either side of the full moon: that was when the squadron's Lysanders took to the air, like strange insects stirring from hibernation.

His course tonight was set for the English Channel and France. At the Channel's narrowest point, France was only twenty miles distant, but tonight he would be crossing at one of the wider stretches, on a bearing just a notch off due south. In the rear-facing cockpit behind him, he had two outbound passengers, both of them French. He did not know their identities. This was standard practice. One was someone he had not encountered before, a man roughly his own age of twenty-two; he was likely to be a member of a French Resistance cell, perhaps a radio operator returning to his country after a spell of training in England.

The other man, twenty or so years older, was someone Archie had transported to and from France several times. A quiet man who said very little and was always courteous. Over time, Archie had formed the impression that he was a political figure of some kind, though not anyone whose face ever appeared in any newspaper report. A man who worked behind the scenes. Perhaps an emissary from de Gaulle himself in London, the exiled leader of the Free French.

Archie's job tonight was to get both men safely to France and himself home in one piece. Usually, these operations were planned so that passengers could be brought back from France on the homeward trip, ensuring maximum value for the risk taken. Not tonight, however; tonight Archie would return home alone. It was perhaps an indication of the importance of the quiet man: he was not someone whose business could wait.

With the moon so bright and not a cloud in the sky, Archie knew he would be able to see the coastline of France from any height, so he took the Lysander up to 8,000 feet. The weather forecast was good, a high-pressure system promising continued perfect visibility. The sea beneath him was like glass, a dark infinity, peaceful and untroubled. On nights like this, a man could think himself a god gazing down from the heavens. A dangerous conceit, for no gods were ever as vulnerable as Archie and his passengers in their lonely little unarmed aircraft.

Nor was that sea beneath him as untroubled as it appeared. He knew that hundreds of ships and landing craft were being massed all along the south coast of England for the Allied invasion of German-occupied

Europe that everyone – including the Germans themselves – knew was coming, sooner now rather than later. Unprecedented quantities of military hardware were being drawn up in readiness, supplemented by fake equipment to deceive German intelligence: dummy aircraft, inflatable tanks, decoy landing craft. Thousands of men were assembling in scores of temporary encampments across England, in training and preparing themselves, rehearsing for the day that would determine the course of the war.

What was not known was when and where the invasion would happen.

Less than an hour into the flight, the French coast came into view. Waves broke against the shore in lazily curling fingers of white foam. Here was more deception, this time on the Germans' part, for all the way along that innocent-looking shoreline lurked the massive bunkers and heavy guns the Germans had installed to repel the anticipated invasion. The long sandy beaches, once beloved by summer holidaymakers, were dense with landmines and a multitude of anti-tank obstacles, many of them hidden underwater. The entire coastline had become a killing zone – known as Hitler's Atlantic Wall.

'Messieurs, la belle France,' Archie announced over the intercom. The younger passenger heard the irony in his tone and gave a snort of bitter amusement. The quiet man said nothing.

Archie checked the time: 2340 hours. He was on track; on this first leg, relying on compass and airspeed, he had covered something over a hundred miles. Off to his left lay Le Havre, heavily defended. To starboard was Ouistreham with its harbour and the canal linking it to Caen; inland beyond it was Caen itself, also well defended. Archie maintained a dead straight bearing between these dangerous points, coming in directly over Cabourg. He held his height at 8,000 feet. Nothing would protect him from the Luftwaffe's night fighters if any were about, but at this height he would be beyond the reach of any light flak the Germans might send up if they were paying attention and spotted him.

And now the second leg of his course would take him deep into the heart of France. Once clear of the coast and the German defences, he dipped the Lysander's nose and descended gently to a couple of thousand feet.

The landscape beneath him was one from which all colour had seeped away, reducing it to a bluish-grey panorama punctuated only by the occasional pinprick of light where someone was being careless with – or perhaps deliberately dismissive of – the Germans' blackout rules.

But absence of colour did not matter; he was not here to enjoy the sylvan beauty of France. What mattered was that in the bright moonlight he could see the land in the detail he needed: its patchwork of fields and even the hedges that divided them, the villages that slipped away beneath him with their clusters of buildings and the spires of churches, here an isolated farmhouse or the bulk of a grand château, there a larger town, the silver surface of a river or lake catching the moonlight, the gleam of a railway line as straight as an arrow or curving gently across the land, a pocket of white mist in a river valley, the dark sections that were forest, and the ribbons of roads, both the routes nationales and the minor roads, the routes départementales, like a network of veins.

All these features were landmarks for him, crucial navigational pinpoints. He was using his maps now, which he had prepared that afternoon by cutting them into strips and folding them so that he could remove them from the map case and hold them in one hand, reading them by the light of that luminous moon. They covered his route with a margin of fifty miles or so in case he should stray off course. The final panes, those that covered his target area, his destination, were at twice the scale, four miles to the inch. His only other navigational aid was an air-reconnaissance photograph of the target area.

And this was where the impossible was called for. With the whole of France sweeping past beneath him, what he was aiming for was a single field in all of that dark expanse: one single field in the immensity of France.

Impossible, but he had done it before, many times. And tonight he did it once more; an hour later, he had found his field. There it was, beneath him. He circled the area to be certain. Yes, there was the crossroads, there to its east was the lake beside the narrow route départementale, running west to east. Enough woodland to provide protection for those who would be meeting him, his reception committee, but still with more than enough flat meadowland for a safe landing. Telegraph poles stood along the side of the road, but none of their cables crossed his landing zone. All matching the photograph. Textbook, he thought.

To climb into the night sky with the moon riding high above him, this was as much an exercise in elegance and beauty as it was war. But war it was, and this was his modest part in that war. This was his corner in that fight, the finding of this one small field. The university air squadron had been his training ground; he had worked hard to put that training to good use. So the pleasure he felt at his achievement was not based on vanity or self-satisfaction, it was knowing that this was the thing he could do. This was his talent, his contribution.

He clicked the intercom again.

'Messieurs, préparez-vous, s'il vous plaît. Nous arrivons.'

He circled the area again to check that all was as it should be. He knew that on the ground, the reception committee would have heard his engine as he approached, so the manoeuvre served the additional purpose of giving them time to emerge from hiding and signal their readiness.

As he completed his loop, a light on the ground – nothing more sophisticated than someone holding a flashlight or a cycle lamp – flashed the correct recognition letter for their part of the operation: three long Morse dashes for O. He pressed his signalling key and responded with his own recognition letter: dash–dot–dash for K.

Now three lights appeared in the field, not blinking this time but steady. They would be ordinary flashlights mounted on sticks about three feet long and angled upward. They formed an inverted capital letter L and marked his landing path, a flarepath in miniature.

If the agent on the ground had done his work correctly, in the way in which he had been trained in England by Archie and his fellow pilots, he would have searched out a field that was clear of tree stumps, boulders and other obstructions, the ground firm and dry and not ruptured by ditches or cart tracks. Soft mud was the worst thing; it could lie in pockets and suck the Lysander's wheels into its grip. The agent had to walk every yard of the landing and taxi path.

Importantly also, Archie could see that tonight's field was not encroached upon too closely by those pieces of woodland, another critical factor in ensuring he could make a safe descent and landing, as well as an equally safe departure. It all boded well.

He came down over the first light, at the beginning of the long leg of the inverted L, at about 70 mph, wing slats out automatically, flaps down and with minimal throttle, and touched down perfectly.

He cut the throttle and braked, gently and steadily at first as he took the feel of the ground. It seemed firm and reasonably even; he caught a glimpse of dry stubble. He increased his braking as he covered the 150 yards towards the second light, the one at the corner of the L. As his port wing passed over the light, he turned briskly to starboard, towards the third light, where he turned once again and taxied back towards the first light.

This was where the reception team had now gathered, a group of shadowy figures. They were armed; he saw the glint of moonlight on steel. When he reached them, he made his final turn so that he was facing the same direction in which he had come down to the field. This positioned him for take-off, facing into the wind, if there was any.

As soon as he came to a stop and gave the thumbs-up sign, a burst of activity got under way. Speed was of the essence. The local agent, the man on the ground, whom he knew only by his code name of Armand, swung himself up towards the cockpit. Archie slid back the roof. His hand remained on the .38 revolver on which it had rested since touchdown.

'Change of plan, mon ami,' Armand called over the noise of the engine. 'You have a passenger to take to England. Don't worry – it's been agreed.'

Such unplanned changes did happen occasionally. When an operation was under way, it was not always possible or wise to contact a pilot to advise him; it was too dangerous to break radio silence.

Over Armand's shoulder, Archie saw that a man was standing off to one side from the others. A quick decision was required, and it was for the pilot alone to make it; he had total authority. How did Archie know this was not a trap or that the man was not a German spy? How did he know Armand had not been turned? For that matter, how did he know the passengers he had brought here were not about to fall straight into the hands of the Gestapo – and himself with them?

The answer was that he did not know any of these things. All the precautions in the world could be taken, but in the end, everything came down to trust and judgement: to two men in a field in France in the loneliest hours of the night, one deciding whether to trust the other, searching for the truth in the other's face in the moonlight.

Archie nodded to indicate that he would take the unplanned passenger. He let go of the revolver. Armand clapped his shoulder, perhaps guessing at the presence of the weapon and certainly understanding the fine balance of the decision, and they shook hands.

'Bonne chance, mon ami.'

Archie turned his attention to his cockpit drill so that he would be ready for a prompt take-off. He kept the engine running.

He was aware that in the passenger cockpit behind him, the quiet man was already unlocking and opening the roof. He knew the ropes. Armand helped him and his companion to free themselves from their leather flying helmets and parachute harnesses, then climb down the ladder that was fixed to the port side of the aircraft.

The number 7 was chalked beside the ladder; Archie knew that Armand would check that seven pieces of luggage were unloaded – namely four small suitcases and three packages. If there was luggage for the return flight, the 7 would be erased and replaced.

But tonight the number 7 was simply erased, with no replacement: the unexpected passenger for Archie's homeward trip had no luggage. He came forward and quickly climbed the ladder to the rear cockpit. Armand settled him into the seat and sorted out his harness and helmet.

Across the field, Archie's inbound passengers and Armand's team were already disappearing into the night.

Archie checked his watch, an RAF-issue Omega pilot's timepiece. Since touchdown, no more than three minutes had passed. His work here was done. He completed his take-off checks, raised a hand in farewell to Armand, and moments later the Lysander was back in the air and heading for home.

Textbook.

Except this was the moment when the textbook fell to pieces.

He heard the unmistakable rattle of machine-gun fire beneath him. It could mean only one thing – a German unit had arrived, either by sheer bad luck or because the operation had been betrayed. He glanced back at the field. The lights marking his landing and take-off path were still in place; Armand had not had time to remove them. They were supplemented now by other lights – muzzle flashes as a machine gun barked again. Another weapon joined in, then another and another, whether in support or opposition.

Archie knew he could do nothing about what was

happening down there. But he also knew that it would not be confined to ground level – someone would want to bring the Lysander down, not only because it was an enemy aircraft but because the Germans were desperate to know how these operations worked and whether special equipment was involved. He had to get as far away as possible as quickly as possible, out of range of the guns.

He pressed forward at full throttle, making the aircraft weave and twist. This was safer than trying to climb out of trouble: the Lysander was a wonderful machine but not a fast climber. He hoped its matte black paintwork would provide a degree of invisibility against the night sky, even with that full moon. But at any moment, he expected to feel the thud of bullets raking the aircraft.

It seemed to take forever before he felt they were out of danger, although in reality it was probably no more than a minute. He took the Lysander up to 2,000 feet and checked his maps to see how much he had deviated from his homeward course, got his bearings and made the necessary corrections. The aircraft responded normally, but nonetheless he tested the flying controls to ensure that nothing had been damaged, then checked propeller pitch, oil and fuel levels, oil pressure, magneto switches. Everything seemed fine.

His thoughts were with Armand and the others as he continued on his course. What had become of them? What had become of the quiet man and the younger man? From time to time, he exchanged a few words with his passenger, although neither of them made any mention of what had happened; there was nothing to be said.

The passenger himself sounded shaken but seemed calm enough.

They were clear of Caen and were making for Cabourg when, inexplicably, the Lysander began veering to the left. Nothing Archie tried would correct the problem. The German bullets had inflicted damage after all.

The intercom crackled. His passenger was saying something, but his voice was weak and his words were unclear. Archie was still busy struggling to make the Lysander respond. He turned in his seat as much as was possible in his bulky flying jacket in the cramped space, but all he could see was the back of the man's head in his flying helmet. He was not moving. Archie called him several times on the intercom, but the man was silent.

Archie brought his attention back to the aircraft and the landscape below. What he saw was not good. They were heading west – entirely the wrong direction – were now following the Normandy coastline on their right and crossing the twin silver ribbons of the Orne river and the Caen canal at Ouistreham. A minute later they passed over Douvres. They could hardly be in a more dangerous location: they were right in the heavily defended killing zone of the Atlantic Wall. At any moment they might find themselves caught by searchlight beams and in the sights of an anti-aircraft battery, or a German night fighter might swoop down to finish them off.

Fate had not yet done with them, however. As Archie continued to wrestle with the Lysander's controls, the engine spluttered, caught again, spluttered some more – and died. All power was gone.

The problem could not be shortage of fuel. The aircraft was fitted with an auxiliary tank carrying an extra 150 gallons added to the inboard tank's 98 – more than adequate for the night's operation – and the gauge said there was plenty of fuel left. So there was no leak, at least not a serious one.

Archie scanned the instrument panel. None of the gauges provided any clues.

Already he was down to 1,000 feet and continuing to lose height. The only positive was that he had regained enough control of the aircraft to maintain a forward direction. He still had no idea what the problem was, but it was irrelevant now – it was time to look for somewhere to put down. He would be making a forced landing on enemy territory: every pilot's nightmare. Worse than that, a forced landing without power.

And there was still the risk of a German fighter picking them off – with no possibility of evasive action of any kind on Archie's part.

He was at 400 feet now, still high enough to clear hazards such as church spires and wireless masts, but that margin of safety would not last long. The Lysander was gliding steadily to earth. The land beneath him was an intricate pattern of fields of interlocking shapes and sizes, some ploughed, some with crops, some meadowland. There would be no Armand to choose a good field for him or set out a landing path. All he could do was land in the best way he could manage and hope for a firm surface devoid of obstacles.

But he saw something else as he descended. Here and there along the coast, massive shapes reared from the darkness, picked out by the moonlight – they were the bunkers, gun emplacements and radar stations of the Atlantic Wall. He had never passed as close to them before. He could even see the rolls of barbed wire and the tank traps, the so-called hedgehogs and dragons' teeth, all along the beaches.

He had no time to dwell on the sight. A dark patch of woodland loomed up ahead of him. Beyond it he saw a good-sized meadow, if he could get that far.

He managed to clear the woodland, but the aircraft continued to lose height, its airspeed falling, and he knew he was out of time and distance. Whatever the condition of the meadow, it would have to do.

He caught a glimpse of white shapes directly ahead on the ground. Cattle? Sheep? They scattered before him. His speed was down to 60 mph, stalling speed even for the Lysander.

He held his breath and put the aircraft down. It bumped up again immediately – he must have hit a deep rut – then the tail came down far too heavily and bounced up again. He had no engine power to deal with it. For a moment he feared the aircraft might tip over, nose first, pinning him and his passenger in their cockpits. But the machine levelled out and continued forward. He braked, not too hard in case there were other ruts whose effect he might exacerbate.

But when he looked up, he saw the dark outline of a large oak tree dead ahead. Probably the only oak tree in this whole meadow, and he had found it.

He had no choice now but to squeeze the brake lever as hard as he could. He skidded and was still braking when the Lysander slammed into the tree.

The noise of the collision was horrendous. He was flung violently forward but managed to stop his head from slamming into the instrument panel. As the aircraft settled amid creaks and groans of protesting metal and wood, he pushed himself back in his seat and moved each of his limbs in turn to check for breaks or fractures, then his feet, hands and neck, and then arched his back.

Everything seemed to be working as it was meant to, and without pain. Still, shock could numb the senses; he would find out soon enough if he really was unscathed.

Then he saw the sight that told him just how much trouble he was in. The Lysander had met the tree at an angle, the great trunk smashing against the aircraft's starboard wing. The wing had been ripped apart. This aircraft would not be taking off again. Ever.

He called out to his passenger but got no reply.

He extricated himself from the cockpit, swung himself across to the ladder and slid open the rear cockpit.

His passenger was dead. He knew that even before he removed the man's flying helmet and saw the glassy eyes staring at nothing. He pressed two fingers to the side of the man's neck, searching for a pulse that he knew was not there.

He drew a deep breath. And gagged immediately at the stench of fuel he sucked in. He dropped to the ground and ran his hand along the auxiliary tank, a torpedo-shaped affair slung beneath the fuselage. His hand came away damp, but a sniff at it told him it was only condensation.

He was about to go to the nose of the aircraft, to investigate there, but a loud hissing noise from that direction indicated what his likely problem was: a broken or detached fuel line. By the sound of it, fuel was spraying out freely – probably a fine spray, which would explain why the fuel gauge had shown no problem.

The question was, where was the fuel spraying? If it hit the hot engine block, the aircraft would become a bomb. The worst thing he could do was open the engine cowling; a sudden rush of air was likely to trigger disaster.

He had to get away from the aircraft. That was plain enough. But there was much to do first. He climbed back up the ladder and released his passenger from the harness. He wrapped both arms about him, grabbing him around the chest and beneath his arms so that he could haul him upright from the seat. The man was heavier than he looked, and there was minimal room for manoeuvre, the structure of the cockpit roof, the bench seat and the jungle of the cabin's interior metalwork being always in the way.

Every second that ticked past was bringing him closer to the explosion that would blow him and this already dead man to kingdom come.

A flurry of movement in the meadow startled him. But it was only those white shapes that had scattered as he came in to land. They turned out to be half a dozen cows, and now they were curious to see what had disrupted their night. They clomped up to the aircraft and watched his efforts, snuffling their disapproval. He hoped there was no protective bull nearby.

Eventually, he was able to drape the upper part of the man's body over the side of the fuselage. He tugged and pushed at it until the corpse's own weight made it slip clear and fall to the ground. It landed with a sickening thud. The cows drew back in alarm.

Archie had seen the mess of blood where the bullet that killed the man had entered his stomach. He must have been in great pain but had known there was nothing Archie could do for him. He had probably bled to death. A lonely death, yet with Archie only a few feet away.

Now Archie leaned across to his own cockpit and retrieved his revolver plus the little carton of bullets he carried, his maps for the operation, and a small tin box.

He climbed down from the aircraft, took another quick look at the dead man's bullet wound, turned him over to check by both sight and feel that the bullet had not exited – this was no time to be squeamish – removed his own flying jacket and shot a hole in what he hoped was roughly the right place in the front of the garment. The alarmed cows withdrew further.

He removed the Omega from his wrist and put it on the dead man's wrist. There was no watch for him to take in exchange. Then he worked the man's arms into the sleeves of the flying jacket.

In preparing for tonight's operation – that period of calm in Tangmere that now seemed a lifetime ago – he had followed his usual practice of dressing in a combination of flying gear and civilian clothes precisely in case he ended up stuck in France: black roll-neck sweater, ordinary trousers, both of these items devoid of manufacturers' marks or labels, as was his underwear. All had seen better days, as would be the case for any French citizen's clothing after years of making do under German occupation.

The tin box contained his escape kit. He knew what was in it: a packet containing twenty thousand francs in paper notes, all genuine, no forgeries – equivalent to about £100, a generous amount – two black-and-white photographs of him that could be used in the preparation of false identity papers, a map of France printed on fine silk so that it could be folded away in the tiniest of spaces, a compass, a fishing line and hook, a penknife, some medical essentials. The map would supplement his own more detailed maps.

What the kit did not contain was a suicide capsule; he had thrown it away long ago.

He wanted to stop now, part of his mind screaming at

him to be off, but he knew he had to be thorough. His final task was to search the dead man's pockets. He found an identity card and some cash, a mix of paper and coins. He took everything. Maybe the identity card was genuine, maybe not. As far as he could tell in the moonlight, the photograph bore only an approximate likeness to himself, but the basics seemed to match. Certainly they offered no glaring contradictions: dark hair, clean shaven, right age. So the card might serve in an emergency. He saw the man's name, Loïc Boiteux, and offered him an apology for the way in which he was being treated in death.

'It's in a good cause, Loïc. You'd approve.'

And now he finally did what the sane part of his mind had been screaming for: he ran. Cowpats burst beneath his feet, but he was oblivious. The cattle saw him coming and bolted ahead of him, their hooves drumming.

He had covered only twenty or thirty strides when the Lysander exploded. The blast threw him to the ground as if he was a child's doll. He had seen a Lysander explode once before, a badly damaged aircraft that had crashlanded at Tangmere. But that aircraft had been almost out of fuel. The manner of its demise was as nothing compared with the inferno that Archie witnessed now. There were two distinct explosions a heartbeat apart as the two fuel tanks went up. An enormous fireball, vivid in shades of red and orange and yellow against the night sky, enveloped the aircraft and the tree. Deadly chunks of flying metal and pieces of the oak tree flew overhead, some screeching like bullet rounds. Archie kept his head down; it was a miracle that none of the debris struck him. The cows, lowing madly in terror, seemed to be equally fortunate.

Within seconds the aircraft was a black husk at the

heart of the blaze. All the oxygen seemed to be sucked from the atmosphere, leaving Archie fighting for breath. And now the flames were engulfing Loïc's body.

Archie knew that the German presence in the area was certain to be heavy, but he did not know how close the nearest Germans were or how long it might take them to get here – it might be only minutes.

But he had arranged things as best he could. What they would find would be the charred remains of the Lysander and its apparent pilot, his body thrown from the aircraft at the moment of impact or as the aircraft exploded. Any discrepancy between Loïc's fatal wound and that bullet hole in the flying jacket would be impossible to detect – if anything even remained of the jacket. Powder burn on the jacket from the revolver's point-blank shot would be obliterated. With any luck, the fact that Loïc was not wearing flying boots would not be noticed – assuming that anything of the man's footwear was even left.

The result was that the Germans would not feel any need to send out search parties to look for the Lysander's pilot. At the very least, Archie's efforts might stall them for a while, buying him valuable time. At any rate, that was what he hoped.

He picked himself up and made for the woodland he had glided over on his landing approach. As he ran, he assessed the state of his body again, his limbs and spine; everything still seemed to be in good working order.

When he was deep enough among the trees to feel reasonably safe from any patrolling squads of Germans or those who might be on their way to the crash site, he spread out his maps in a patch of moonlight. As he did so, there was a moment when the wind changed direction, and over the crackle of the flames devouring the Lysander he heard the rise and fall of the surf. It was a reminder of how close he was to the coast. He traced as accurately as he could the route the Lysander had followed on its troubled descent and identified where he believed he was now.

The standing advice for pilots stranded in enemy territory was to find a Catholic priest and put themselves in his hands. This was wiser than trusting local people, went the rationale. There was no way of knowing who among the ordinary population would risk helping a stranded British pilot, the penalty for doing so being summary execution.

And there was the danger posed by collaborators or those who simply wanted to get into the Germans' good books – these were the ones who would not only turn him away but would also report his whereabouts. Worst of all, they might take him into their homes, letting him think he was safe, only to hand him over.

Most French priests were opposed to the war and the occupation, and so were generally considered a safer bet. Some would also have contacts in the Resistance and access to the secret escape networks by which pilots could be returned to England. In the end, this too was a gamble, of course – there was no guarantee that all priests could be trusted – but it was his best chance.

So he needed to find a priest. Which meant he needed to find a church.

He searched the map panes for the little symbol with a cross that represented a church. The panes offered an incomplete picture because he was never meant to be in this particular area, but he was able to identify several possibilities. The nearest of them lay southwest of him, in a tiny village called Belville. So Belville would be his destination. Belville would be where he pinned his hopes.

He folded the maps, prised open the escape kit, took out the compass and set off. The sound of the surf rose and fell but was always there. He thought about the dark silhouettes he had glimpsed as the Lysander fell to earth and about the German patrols that would be guarding them, and he avoided the roads as far as possible, keeping to the edges of fields rather than cutting through them. The result was a zigzag route that increased the distance he would have to travel, doubling or even tripling it, but it meant he always had the cover of hedges and ditches and trees. That cover was vital. The moonlight, formerly a good friend to him, could endanger him now – not only because of the Germans but also because of French civilians who had been woken by the crash and explosion and might now be watching these fields.

He regretted the loss of the Omega. Even tracking the moon's passage across the sky, it was hard to gauge time. So he was not sure how long he had been on the move when he heard the distant thrumming of a vehicle engine.

He stopped to listen. It was definitely drawing closer. On the skyline, he glimpsed an intermittent flicker of light. It had to be from headlight beams. Calling the map to mind, he figured that the vehicle was on a minor road that would bring it right to where he was and along the other side of the wire fence he was presently following.

It might be looking for the crashed Lysander, or it might simply be a routine patrol. But for the moment, moving off in any direction would be too risky; he did not know which direction would be safe. He would have to wait until the vehicle had either passed him by or changed direction completely and gone away.

He crawled into the undergrowth on his side of the fence and pressed himself flat on the ground. It was an exercise in passivity and he hated it. Going nowhere, doing nothing, waiting to be captured. Pinned to the earth by gravity and fear. No majestic sky about him, no moon guiding him.

The engine noise grew louder. The vehicle was not changing direction, it was not going away; it was coming right at him, and in fact he was hearing not one but two vehicles – lorries or trucks, he reckoned.

Now they were upon him, right on the other side of the fence, mere yards away, so close that their masked headlight beams washed over him.

The hiss and chatter of radio traffic rose and fell in two separate waves as the vehicles passed. German voices called out excitedly. There was laughter. Some enthusiastic Sieg Heils rang out. He guessed that the occupants of the lorries had caught their first sight of the flames of the burning Lysander in the distance.

But there seemed to be no note of surprise in the voices or laughter. These troopers had known the aircraft was there; they had come looking for it. Looking for him.

The word was out: unless his efforts to pass Loïc off as the pilot of the Lysander were successful, he was a hunted man, a fugitive. For the enthusiastic troopers, this was a night's sport, a hunting expedition. And it was one in which Archie had to hope he could avoid being the quarry.

If his luck held.

Oberleutnant Heinrich Hauser was in a hurry. He thrashed his little camouflage-liveried Kübelwagen along the lanes and narrow roads that led from Belville and his beloved Marie. A bright full moon hung above him in a cloudless sky; all the stars in the universe seemed to be on display.

The further east he travelled, the closer he came to the coast. The whine of the Kübel's engine drowned the beat of the surf, but he could sense its steady rhythm, like an eternal echo that was always there. The sound was louder at night. Often, he could hear it in the yard behind Marie's little cottage. He was fascinated by it; he who had grown up in the back streets and tenements of Berlin and had never seen an ocean until the Wehrmacht sent him to France.

The Wehrmacht was his family. But only the Wehrmacht. Never Hitler's Reich.

Despite his hurry, from time to time he had to stop at a fixed checkpoint or was flagged down by a mobile patrol. Security was particularly tight in this area because of the Atlantic Wall. Civilian vehicles, few and far between anyway given the unavailability of fuel, were completely forbidden, and even military vehicles required a high-level official pass. Heinrich had such a pass – he had a way of obtaining passes for most eventualities – and he was well known to most of the troopers manning the barriers or crammed into their sweaty patrol trucks.

Usually when he made this journey, which he did frequently, he would exchange a few friendly words with the bored troopers – 'Everything quiet here, men?' 'Yes, all quiet, Herr Oberleutnant!' 'No little mademoiselles hidden away in your truck?' 'Not tonight, Herr Oberleutnant!' – and then he would continue on his way.

His heart was always with the ordinary men.

But tonight things were a little different. Tonight the young troopers were on edge; their talk was all about the explosion.

'Did you hear it, Herr Oberleutnant?'

'I heard it.'

'Could you tell where it was?'

'No. Could you?'

'It was over that way, Herr Oberleutnant –'

'He's wrong, Herr Oberleutnant, ignore him – it was over in this direction.'

'But what was it, Herr Oberleutnant? That's what we all want to know.'

He confessed he did not know. He was going to try to find out. He listened to their guesswork. Sometimes that was all these men really wanted: to be listened to. The explosion was too big for a mortar round, someone said. A bomb from an aircraft? Maybe, but why only one? Or maybe it was the accidental detonation of blasting material left over from carving out chunks of rock when the bunkers and the gun emplacements of the Atlantic Wall were being built.

'Herr Oberleutnant, what if it's the start of the enemy invasion? What if the English Tommies are coming?'

'No need to lose sleep over that, soldier,' was Heinrich's brusque reply. To allow men listening time was one thing, but potentially alarmist talk had to be nipped in the bud.

'There won't be any invasion. No English Tommies. That's why we have our Atlantic Wall – to make sure that doesn't happen. That's why you and your courageous comrades are here to stop spies and saboteurs getting up to mischief. The enemy wouldn't stand a chance and he knows it. You'll see to that. So no more treasonable talk about English Tommies. Your work is important to the Reich. Stay on your toes and do your duty.'

And having thus fulfilled his own duty to the Reich – for Oberleutnant Heinrich Hauser was always to be seen as its loyal servant – he resumed his urgent journey.

But his mind kept returning to Marie. She would not let him go. She was everywhere, all around him. He had the scent of her in the night air, the feel of her arms about him, the taste of her in the salt ocean breeze that blew across the dunes. He lit a cigarette to settle his nerves and regain a proper focus.

'Pull yourself together, Hauser!'

The nicotine kicked in. He engaged gear, rammed his foot to the floor and accelerated away, drawing so hungrily on the cigarette that the hot tobacco stung his lips.

His destination was the garrison headquarters and regional Kommandantur located in the handsome Château de Tailleville, northwest of Douvres. It was familiar territory to him: not only his military base but also his most important marketplace. Who here did not know Heinrich Hauser? Who among them did not do a little business with him from time to time in discreet corners? Officers and regular troopers, they were all one to him as long as they had cash in their pockets to fund their hearts' desires. Or their lovers' desires, more often than not. It was a democracy of commerce, possibly the most honest thing the mighty German Reich had to offer. The notion pleased him. Pity it had taken war to bring it about.

But tonight he found Tailleville in a state of tension

and confusion. As with the jittery troopers on the lonely roads, it was all to do with the explosion. No one he quizzed as he made his way through the building's warren of corridors and offices knew anything for certain about it; everything was speculation and guesswork. People bustled past on all sides, uniformed clerks rushed from room to room on whatever errands had been entrusted to them, duty officers yelled into telephones. Everyone seemed to be talking and shouting over everyone else as if volume alone might produce the answers they needed.

He found Major Gerhard Naumann in his office at the rear of the building. Here, thankfully, things were quiet. Naumann beckoned him in as soon as he arrived. Heinrich entered and closed the door. Naumann was studying the large wall map of the area. He was by profession a historian, having been a teacher before being called up. He returned Heinrich's salute. By habit and unspoken agreement, here in the privacy of the major's office, it was a traditional Wehrmacht salute, not the despised Nazi one.

Naumann opened a drawer of his desk, took out two glasses and a bottle of Armagnac, and poured a measure into each glass. He had bought the Armagnac from Heinrich at a good price – good for both of them and therefore what Heinrich considered a fair price. Naumann was one of his best customers. And Heinrich knew he was Naumann's most trusted officer. Their regular business transactions only served to strengthen that trust.

They clinked glasses and drank. In accordance with another of their customs, there was no spoken toast: that was a private matter for each man, according to his personal hopes or demons.

Heinrich knew what Naumann's toast would be. People told Heinrich things; they confessed their little secrets to him in those discreet corners where their business was transacted. The major had a sick wife back home in Hanover. Sick and probably dying. Naumann's heart's desire was to be with her.

As for Heinrich, his silent toast was to Marie.

'I wasn't expecting to see you, Heinrich. You're not on duty tonight.'

'Yet here I am, Herr Major. I couldn't ignore that explosion. I can have my men ready in the blink of an eye if they're needed.'

'Good man. I knew I could count on you. In fact, I was thinking of sending to the barracks for you.'

Heinrich said nothing. No need for the major to know that his favourite officer would not have been found in the barracks. That was why Heinrich had raced to be here. Romantic and sexual relationships with the local female population were accepted as a normal part of occupation life, but spending entire nights away from barracks, as had become Heinrich's regular practice, was frowned upon up the chain of command. Even easy-going Gerhard Naumann would have difficulty with that – even in relation to Heinrich.

It turned out that the major was as much in the dark about the explosion as everyone else in Tailleville.

'It seems that an aircraft – possibly an enemy aircraft – has come down somewhere west of here. Following the explosion, we had a report of a crashed aircraft from a local farmer, the owner of the land where it came down – if the report is true. So far, we haven't been able to confirm his report from any other source, and we don't know if the aircraft crashed of its own accord – possibly trying to land – or was shot down. We don't know which direction it was travelling, or whether it's a fighter or a bomber.'

'A solitary bomber would be very unusual, Herr Major. But it might have been a reconnaissance aircraft undertaking an assessment of the Wall. It wouldn't be the first time that has happened.'

'My thought exactly. Or it might have been probing our defences, testing them. The two squads of troopers I've already dispatched are checking the location the farmer reported. In the meantime, we're contacting other Wehrmacht units in search of hard information. There are plenty of patrols out there – someone must have seen something. Failing that, even reports from reliable civilian informers would be welcome.'

'If an anti-aircraft battery brought the aircraft down, someone must know.'

Naumann looked unhappy. 'That's one of the many things we're trying to find out.'

Heinrich sipped his Armagnac. 'The aircraft could have continued flying for a distance after being hit – an unknown distance, so it's impossible to say where the anti-aircraft battery might be located.'

Naumann sighed. 'And we don't actually know for sure if it *is* an enemy aircraft. It might be one of our own, perhaps a night fighter on patrol. But the skies have been quiet tonight, with no airborne skirmishes. If it's a Luftwaffe fighter, perhaps pilot error or a technical malfunction brought it down. So we're also contacting Luftwaffe bases to see if an aircraft is missing.'

'In that case, it could have come from almost anywhere in France. Herr Major, with respect, you may be trying to find a needle in a haystack.'

Naumann nodded wearily in agreement. He removed his spectacles and compressed the bridge of his nose between finger and thumb. Heinrich knew he had sinus problems.

'You're right, Heinrich, of course. But it could be a very important needle. If it's an enemy aircraft, it might have been delivering or collecting foreign agents or Resistance personnel. And if there are any survivors of the crash –'

Heinrich finished the sentence for him. 'We want those survivors. We want any intelligence we can get from them.'

'Exactly.' Naumann massaged his nose again. 'There's one further thing.'

At once Heinrich was on his guard. He sensed the major's uneasiness. Something other than the matter of locating and identifying the mystery aircraft was troubling him.

'Herr Major?'

Naumann's gaze was on the map. 'Someone's on his way from Caen to join us.' He paused. 'To help us, I'm told.'

'Do we need help, Herr Major?'

'It would be wise in this case to accept it.' Naumann put his spectacles back on and consulted a piece of paper. 'His name is Klemt. Friedrich Klemt. He's a major in the Gestapo.'

Heinrich felt a tiny quiver of anxiety. An unnecessary anxiety, no doubt.

'We're honoured,' he said. 'What help will this Major Klemt provide, I wonder?'

'Apparently, he has a particular interest in partisan and Resistance operations and is an expert interrogator.'

'I see. Meaning more expert than we are. Well, I'm sure he'll be an asset – provided we actually have someone for him to interrogate. It seems a little odd, don't you think?'

'What does?'

'I don't doubt his expertise. But he may be wasting his time coming here at this stage. Why not wait until we locate the aircraft and establish whether there are survivors? Wouldn't that make better sense?'

Naumann sighed. 'Maybe so, Heinrich. I don't know. It's not given to me to understand how Gestapo minds work.'

He handed Heinrich a note of map references for where, supposedly, the aircraft was to be found.

Heinrich knocked back the last of his Armagnac and saluted again. He had his briefing. But a briefing that raised more questions than it answered.

A Gestapo man stirring himself to come here from Caen on the off-chance there might be a foreign agent or a member of the Resistance for him to interrogate? And not even waiting to see if such a person had been apprehended?

Really?

And Heinrich could tell that Naumann was asking himself the same question.

What was this Major Friedrich Klemt really after?

Three-quarters of an hour later, Heinrich was picking his way across an isolated meadow, flashlight in hand as he tried to avoid the deposits of cow dung that seemed to be everywhere, lurking where the moonlight could not find them. It was impossible; every third or fourth step had him squelching through the soft crusts. His troopers followed behind him, their colourful language confirming they were having no better luck. The animals who had deposited the disgusting things watched the goings-on, lowing occasionally as though enjoying their revenge on these intruders who had come to disturb them – their second bout of disturbance tonight, Heinrich realised.

The squads that Naumann had sent ahead of him had found the aircraft exactly where the French farmer had said. They had radioed Tailleville accordingly, and it had passed the information to Heinrich. As it turned out, the crash site was only about thirty kilometres from Belville. Little wonder the explosion had woken him.

He caught the smell of the wreck long before he saw it, the sour stink of burning and aircraft fuel contaminating the atmosphere of the whole meadow. All that was left now was a charred shell from which curls of smoke were still rising. A propeller blade was missing and the fuselage had been broken into pieces by the force of the blast, one wing crushed and folded about a large oak tree.

He saw at once that the aircraft was a Lysander – the almost mythical aircraft used by the RAF to ferry spies and Resistance operatives to and from France because of its ability to land in and take off from almost any small field. He had never seen one before, except in blurred training photographs, but there was no mistaking the high-mounted wings and the clumsy snub nose.

The other squads had fanned out and were checking the hedgerows and undergrowth for anyone alive or dead. A sour-faced Bavarian called Mannstein, the same rank as Heinrich but in his forties a decade older, had stayed behind, his only apparent duty being to guard the badly burned corpse of a man that had been found beside the smoking hulk.

'The pilot,' Mannstein confidently informed Heinrich.

Heinrich shone his flashlight full in Mannstein's face. The man always reminded him of a tortoise, with his wrinkled bald pate and little eyes that were now blinking blearily against the light as though Heinrich had just woken him. Heinrich had never liked him, and the sentiment was mutual. The Bavarian knew about Marie and Heinrich. He knew about Heinrich's absences from barracks. Heinrich had a hunch that Mannstein had made a pass at Marie more than once and been rebuffed. Marie refused to speak of the matter. Sweet Marie, who never hurt a fly, who never had an unkind thought and never wanted to criticise anyone.

'The pilot,' repeated the Bavarian. 'Definitely.'

Heinrich came closer with the flashlight. 'Who says?'

Mannstein pushed the flashlight away and directed it at the corpse. 'See for yourself. Flying helmet, flying jacket, fancy wristwatch – now *there*'s a souvenir worth having! He's the pilot all right.'

'You've searched him?'

'Of course. And found nothing.'

'No ID?'

'Nothing. Didn't I just say?'

Heinrich thought for a moment. The skill with which the Lysander pilots navigated was the stuff of legend, how they had developed a unique way of operating in the period of a full moon – on nights such as tonight – with, it was said, nothing more than maps and compass.

'Any maps?' he asked.

'None.' Mannstein hesitated. 'Well, none on the body from what I could see. Everything's all burned up.'

'What about the cockpits? Did you check them?'

Mannstein shook his wrinkled head. A tortoise indeed.

'Couldn't get up there,' he said. 'Everything's still too hot to touch – the fire was just dying down as we got here.'

'Any sign of a weapon on the corpse? A handgun?'

Mannstein shook his head again and yawned.

'Why are you guarding the body? Afraid it might run off?'

'Wild animals. It has to be kept safe. We've been ordered to take it to the medical unit, to the morgue. The medical officer wants it. Don't ask me why.'

'Wild animals? What wild animals? Cows?'

'Very funny, Hauser.'

The man was simply too lazy to search properly; that was the truth of the matter. But someone had to cover all the angles, all the possibilities. If not Heinrich, it would be someone else. Better it should be Heinrich. That way, he stood a better chance of retaining control of the situation.

'Get out of the way, Mannstein.'

Heinrich crouched down beside the dead man. He tried not to look at the blackened skull with its bits of roasted flesh. He forced himself not to retch at the smell. He gritted his teeth and went through all the pockets of the man's trousers and flying jacket, some sections of which were so burned that they crumbled to ashes at the touch of his gauntleted hand: gallingly, he found nothing, just as Mannstein had said.

The contents of several troopers' water bottles cooled the ladder sufficiently to allow Heinrich to climb up and investigate both cockpits. Mannstein watched.

'Why not get one of your men to do that?' he said.

'Because I'm not like you, Mannstein.'

When Heinrich bent into the cockpits, the air was

barely breathable; it instantly coated his mouth and nostrils with an oily residue. He had to keep surfacing to fill his lungs with air that was in any case only fractionally cleaner.

Again, he found nothing. The map case had survived the fire but was empty even of ashes.

He set his troopers to a close-quarters flashlight search of the ground beneath and in the vicinity of the aircraft. Zero result yet again.

But perhaps zero *was* a result. Once again, better for him to recognise that and act on it than someone else.

'It's too convenient, Mannstein, too neat and perfect. It feels like someone methodically stripped this man and the aircraft of everything that could be of use to us. Lysanders aren't fighter aircraft; they're usually unarmed, but what kind of pilot flies into enemy-held territory without a personal sidearm, a pistol, for self-defence? Would you do that?'

Mannstein shrugged. 'I'm not a pilot.'

'Well, here's something else. If you *were* a pilot, you'd have an escape kit – knife, compass, matches, water purifying tablets, cash. Where's this man's escape kit? Strange that it should vanish, just like everything else. And maps – don't you find it suspicious that not a single fragment of a map has survived? No, Mannstein, the maps weren't destroyed by fire – they were removed *before* the explosion and fire by whoever left this dead man here to fool us. A decoy. Well, it hasn't worked; the trick hasn't fooled us. At least, it hasn't fooled me. You think this is the pilot? I think you're wrong.'

He prodded the corpse with the toe of his boot, kicking one of its feet – not a hard blow, an absent-minded action rather than a violent or angry one. A small cloud of dust drifted up through the beam of his flashlight.

Then he saw something. He crouched down again.

Like the rest of the dead man's body, both feet were badly burned, their footwear almost to the point of disintegration. But what could just be made out was that the footwear was a pair of ordinary civilian shoes. Not flying boots. Shoes.

The pilot – the *real* pilot, as Heinrich now believed – had taken a chance that the footwear would be totally consumed in the blaze. That gamble had not paid off. The truth would be discovered soon enough by the medical officer. Once again, therefore, better for Heinrich to step in and take the credit.

'That settles it,' he told Mannstein. 'This man wasn't the pilot, he was a passenger. The pilot's on the run somewhere out there.' He nodded towards the moonlit countryside. 'The maps are gone not only to deny them to us but because he needs them. He'll have the escape kit as well. He may be alone, or there may be another passenger who's now on the run with him. We should assume he's armed – that missing pistol. He may be wounded, but that won't make him any less dangerous. He has the whole countryside to hide in – woodland, hedgerows, ditches, any patch of brambles or bushes big enough to conceal him – or he might take refuge in a barn, a byre, a shed, even a farmhouse if he comes across anyone stupid enough to shelter him.'

A look of alarm passed across Mannstein's face; the Bavarian sensed that a task of some kind was on the way, something more daunting than watching over a dead man. Something that might even involve danger. His wizened tortoise head drew back as if seeking the safety of a

38

protective shell.

'Hauser, since you know so much, what are you saying we should do?'

'The odds are in our favour tonight, but they won't stay that way for long. If he has fake ID, he can travel from here if he's fit to do so. He probably has cash, so he might even chance the trains in the morning if he's bold enough – and if he does that, we'll lose him. If he manages to make contact with a Resistance group, same result – we'll lose him. That's how the odds can swing against us. Tonight is our best chance to catch him. We have three squads out here. I propose we agree on a search zone and divide it between us.'

The Bavarian nodded without enthusiasm.

It was a good plan, Heinrich reckoned, one that was worthy of a shrewd Wehrmacht officer, astute and alert.

'And by the way, Mannstein.'

'What?'

'Don't even think about helping yourself to that wristwatch.'

The Bavarian shot him a filthy look. Which was fine by Heinrich. He commandeered more water bottles and looked for a tussock of grass with which to clean the cow dung from his boots.

And wondered what he should do if he actually found the missing pilot.

God forbid.

Archie's luck did not hold.

For a time, all seemed well. The lorries with the excited troopers on board passed him by and he pressed on across the fields. The strategy of following their perimeter made for a slow back-and-forth progress, but he stuck with it. The sky remained cloudless, so as well as his compass he had the path of the moon to ensure he was always following a southwesterly bearing.

Sometimes he came across well-trodden footpaths. These he took when they followed the direction he wanted, but he was always careful when he did so, for fear of encountering German foot patrols.

From time to time across the fields he saw an isolated cottage or sometimes a cluster of farm buildings. They were clearly visible in the moonlight, though always the dwellings were in darkness. He saw no movement, heard nothing, which suggested that the occupants were fast asleep. Sometimes at first he was tempted to approach, even if only to see if there was a bicycle he could take. But in the end he resisted the temptation.

There were no major roads in the area, only minor ones, and these too he avoided. He was right to do so: now and then he heard vehicle engines and German voices and glimpsed the flicker of masked headlights. Sometimes the vehicles were on the move and sometimes they were stationary, suggesting that roadblocks were in place. He wondered whether they were this area's normal level of security or whether they were there specifically because of him.

Always in the distance was the background rumble of the ocean.

He came to a lane that separated two fields. It was

really no more than a dirt track, two parallel channels of hardened earth with weeds and grass growing along the centre. Crossing the lane would put him out in the open briefly, making him visible beneath that bright moon, or he could stay on his own side of the lane and travel parallel to it until he found a relatively safe crossing point. But how long might that take? And how much of a detour?

He remained crouching for a time in the undergrowth, watching and listening for any movement or indication of German presence – or of anyone else. There was none. A thin mist enveloped the scene. The only sound was the chirr of crickets all around.

He took two paces into the lane.

A shout rang out. Unmistakably a German shout, hoarse and urgent.

'Halt!'

His heart almost stopped. He looked up the lane to his right. Where it had previously been deserted, now a figure had risen from the mist. The man must have been prone on the ground and completely motionless. Now he was on his feet. A second figure appeared beside him, then another. There were more shouts. A searchlight beam cut through the mist; an engine coughed and came to life. A vehicle had been hidden behind a stand of trees at the side of the lane. It was a perfect trap, and he had blundered right into it.

But there was no going back now. Nor could there be any question of shooting his way out of trouble – his revolver would be useless against the Germans' firepower.

He leapt across the lane and pushed through the chest-high bushes on the other side, stumbling into the dry ditch behind them. Beyond the ditch was a field where a leafy crop of some kind was growing, perhaps potatoes. He saw at once that the foliage was too low to provide him with any cover; he would have to stay at the perimeter of the field, in the ditch, turning left to get away from the Germans. The question then would be whether he could outrun them.

The troopers, possibly. But the vehicle? Not a chance.

And besides, turning left and away from the Germans was exactly what they would expect him to do. So he turned not left but right, holding to the ditch and running at a crouch towards them, hoping they would believe they could make their best progress on the lane and would therefore not enter the ditch; not yet anyway, not until he had passed them.

As he ran, he heard a shot fired and felt a sharp blow to the side of his head. The stupid idea occurred to him that it was how being struck by an iron bar would feel. But somewhere else in his mind, there was a different idea, a more realistic one: it was not an iron bar but a bullet that had hit him.

The blow knocked him sideways, but he kept his balance and continued running towards the Germans, separated from them and their vehicle only by the bushes bordering the track. The thought that sustained him now was that he had not been seen by the Germans since he entered the ditch, and in his dark clothing he was well camouflaged. He was fairly sure that the shot that had caught him had been fired more or less at random in his general direction and not because the shooter had seen him and been able to take proper aim. The bushes were too dense for that. In fact, they were so dense that apart from the beam of that searchlight,

42

the vehicle itself was now barely visible to him – which suggested he must be invisible both to it and to the troopers on foot in the lane.

There was another shout, this time one that seemed to be addressed to the running troopers. And there had been no further gunfire. Perhaps someone had decided he was to be taken alive. Not that that would amount to any better an outcome than being gunned down here and now.

The rattle and whine of the German vehicle and the thuds of the troopers running on the hard earth of the lane had grown fainter. He stopped running and chanced a look back, hands propped on knees as he tried to catch his breath. The vehicle was still hidden from his view, but he could see the bobbing steel helmets of the troopers – who were now where he had anticipated they would end up, in the ditch and heading in the direction he had avoided.

So far so good, but now he raised his hand to explore the injury to his head. It was worse than he expected: his hair and neck and the top of his sweater were soaked in blood.

He had to stop the blood loss, otherwise he risked falling unconscious. Already he could feel his body temperature dropping despite the warmth of the night. He knelt down and opened the tin box, the escape kit. Inside he found a length of thin bandage about three inches wide, tightly packed to take up as little space as possible. He unrolled it, folded it over on itself and wound it about his head as tightly as he could.

By the time he finished, he was exhausted. More than anything else in the world, what he wanted to do now was simply lie down and go to sleep.

He did not dare. Give in to that urge and he might as well call out to the Germans and surrender.

He resumed running away from them – if stumbling along half unconscious could be called running.

Heinrich requisitioned a farmhouse with a good-sized yard as an operating base for the search, turning out the farmer and his family and ordering them to seek lodging elsewhere.

'But where do you expect us to go?' objected the farmer. His children clung to their mother and stared up at Heinrich, terror in their sleepy eyes.

'Not my problem,' he replied. 'Just don't get in our way or you'll be shot.'

He watched as the farmer and his family trudged off into the night.

Those sleepy eyes. The fear in them.

He turned to a truck driver.

'Take them to some other farm. Find out if they have family nearby. Take them there if that's what they want.'

Now it was the driver who was staring at him. *Going soft, Hauser?* Words not spoken, but Heinrich heard them all the same.

'What are you waiting for? Off you go, man!'

By late morning it was clear that the search was a failure. After that sighting of the pilot beside the potato field by Heinrich and his squad – a worrying moment – there was no further trace of the man. Somehow he had just melted into thin air.

But things might yet change, of course. Naumann had now deployed almost the entire garrison, a further hundred men, sending them out to supplement the efforts of Heinrich and Mannstein and their squads. With so many men now involved in the hunt, it did not seem humanly possible for the pilot, on foot and presumably without local assistance, to continue to evade capture – especially if he had a bullet wound or had been injured in the crash.

45

Unless he died, of course. Or was already dead by now. That would be one way of resolving the situation once and for all. An unfortunate resolution from the pilot's point of view, admittedly, but still a resolution.

Heinrich reviewed his own position. He had acquitted himself well under tricky circumstances. He had taken opportunities as they presented themselves, making sure no one else could interfere. Even though it would be known that he had missed his chance at the potato field, there would be credit for him from Naumann. He would be acknowledged as the one who had figured out that the pilot had survived the crash, the one who had seen through the attempted decoy ruse with the dead man, the one who had organised the initial search. Without his intervention, that dolt Mannstein would still be standing guard over a corpse and a herd of cows. All of this would be obvious to anyone, in particular Naumann. The major could have no complaint; he would see that Heinrich, his best officer, had, as always, justified his trust in him.

Which was exactly how Heinrich always needed things to be. Perhaps especially now, with a Gestapo man in the offing.

He was chewing over these thoughts, standing in the farmyard as he enjoyed a quiet cigarette and finding his mind returning inevitably to Marie, when a black Mercedes sedan appeared in the distance, racing along the narrow roads in a cloud of dust.

He put all thoughts of Marie from his mind. He dropped his cigarette on the ground and crushed it beneath his boot. A black Mercedes staff car meant only one thing.

'Trouble,' he said, to no one in particular.

A trooper overheard him. 'Herr Oberleutnant?'

'We have company.'

The trooper frowned, not yet understanding.

'Gestapo. Be on your best behaviour. Pass it on. Be quick about it.'

The trooper finished changing the tyre that had blown on the Kübelwagen, then made himself scarce. Heinrich saw him speaking to his comrades. Within seconds, every man in the farmyard would know. No communication network had yet been invented that was better than that between soldier and soldier.

Now that the search zone had expanded so much, Heinrich had given orders for the search's operating base to be relocated. All the paraphernalia of the operation was now being loaded into trucks for transportation to a new location. Munitions, communications hardware, medical supplies, catering equipment and the huge quantities of food necessary for so many men were all being packed up and loaded. Trucks lumbered into and out of the farmyard, their engines revving. The air was blue with exhaust fumes, orders were being barked out on every side, harassed troopers tried not to trip over each other.

The black Mercedes pulled into the farmyard and negotiated its way through this apparent chaos. Everyone gave it a wide berth. It came to a halt. Its driver hurried to open one of the rear doors. Naumann emerged, looking even more unhappy and tense than usual.

The driver opened the door on the other side of the Mercedes. For a few moments nothing happened. Then, as though he had been waiting to make the most of his entrance, out stepped a man as thin as a stick. Skeletal face, high cheekbones, humourless mouth, lips a thin line. A perfect Aryan with his blue eyes and that blonde hair

47

so tightly cropped that his pink scalp showed through. His head swivelled slowly from side to side as he took in the activity in the farmyard and the lines of troopers moving slowly over the fields. Then he donned his uniform cap, shielding that delicate scalp from the sun's rays, clicked his heels together and thrust his right arm towards the sky.

'Heil Hitler!'

Major Friedrich Klemt of the Gestapo had arrived.

Heinrich looked at Naumann. Naumann looked back at him. Klemt's right arm remained aloft, awaiting appropriate responses.

'Heil Hitler!' Heinrich and Naumann chorused in unison, their right arms raised and outstretched.

Heinrich felt sick.

Archie wondered how much more his body could take. He collapsed several times during the night and lay where he fell, unable to continue, or managed to drag himself beneath a hedge or bushes, waiting to see if this would be the moment of his death. His head felt as if someone was tightening the jaws of a huge vice around it. But at least the bleeding seemed to have stopped. Even so, he blacked out several times.

He began to understand that the blackouts were a release that were giving his body a chance to recover. When he came to, he had enough strength to carry on – until his next collapse. There were some tiny Benzedrine tablets in the escape kit. He took only one of them because he did not know how long he might have to make them last. He also wanted to avoid the overconfidence they might create.

His progress through the countryside was far slower than before his injury. Sometimes when he saw a cottage in the distance, he thought again about looking for a bicycle but dismissed the idea as too dangerous. On one occasion, he heard the despairing scream of some small nocturnal creature that had been pounced upon by a predator in the darkness. An owl glided past him, ghostly and silent, no higher than his shoulder. Such moments were reminders that death was never far away, its presence not felt until too late.

Dawn arrived. The moon faded and the sun began to burn off the mist. He saw the occasional farm worker going about their tasks – women at least as often as men, for he knew that France had lost so many from its male workforce, whether captured soldiers locked up in German prisoner-of-war camps or civilians sent to work in German industry.

He stuck to his decision and stayed well away from

dwellings and people alike. He thought no more about bicycles. He drank from streams when he came across them because he did not want to add dehydration to his troubles. He made himself rest even when no blackout spell felt imminent.

The morning was well advanced, the sun high, when at last he saw a spire in the distance. There was no need to check his map – it had to be his objective, the village of Belville. A small flutter of hope rose within him.

But this was not the time to be reckless, so he did not make directly for the village. His energy and strength were draining with each minute, but he made himself hold to his strategy of keeping to the boundaries of fields, where there was cover for him provided he kept well down.

The village comprised several lanes and narrow streets that met at a crossroads. Beyond the crossroads was the grey stone church, his goal. The streets were lined with small whitewashed cottages, each standing on its own piece of land separated from its neighbours and all with a shed or two, a barn or a lean-to outbuilding on their ground.

But something bad had happened here. Something very bad that no map could report. At first he was not even sure if this was still a living village. Many of the little cottages were in ruins, some of them completely destroyed, others gutted by fire and characterised by flaking or smoke-stained paintwork, missing roof tiles and cracked frontages. Half-hearted bits of scaffolding indicated where repair work had been attempted but abandoned, presumably for want of building materials – the Germans would have requisitioned everything. Here and there, ancient pieces of agricultural equipment furred with brown rust were slowly disintegrating into the earth.

But despite everything, this was indeed a living village, for thin wisps of smoke drifted up from some of the chimneys into the still air. He moved forward, another field closer, and heard voices where a window or door was open. He paused again, worried that there might be dogs that would detect him and start to bark.

A dog did bark, but not nearby and not at him. Nor did he feel observed by anyone in any of the cottages. Again, he moved closer. He came along the side of a small barn and at last closed in on the grey stone building of the church.

Only to find that his efforts were all for nothing. The church was just another grim ruin – as were the priest's house that stood beside it and another building that might once have been a small school. The grey walls of the church enclosed only emptiness; broken windows stared coldly back at him like the dead eyes of poor Loïc Boiteux; crows squabbled where prayers had once been offered. Through a missing section of wall he could see that statues of saints and the Virgin lay in dusty fragments. The crucifix and Jesus were in pieces.

There was no priest here. There could not possibly be, for no priest would leave the icons of his faith, the crucified Jesus and the Virgin, the mother of God, in such a state.

There was no one here who could help Archie.

To his shame, he felt tears spring to his eyes. He made no attempt to stop them. So much struggle to get here safely, so much of his failing strength wasted. And all for this, for nothing, for a useless ruin. It felt like a judgement passed on him.

He lay prone in the long grass beside the barn, spent

and helpless, unable to stir himself to movement, unable even to think what to do or where to go now.

Perhaps he slipped from consciousness into sleep – not a collapse like the other times, more like a sleep of exhaustion and despair – but he could not be sure, and that in itself was frightening, for it suggested that his mental systems were seizing up, becoming as unresponsive as the engine of the doomed Lysander.

His head was throbbing, far worse than previously. He could not get past the pain: it blinded him, paralysed him. Even thought was becoming impossible. What if his mind closed down completely?

This cottage behind him, to which the barn belonged: could he risk asking there for refuge?

No. It was an insane notion and he dismissed it at once. How could he possibly do that, after all the caution he had exercised so far?

But what else was there for him? He must go to the cottage. He had no choice. That was the only course open to him now.

No. Again, no. It was out of the question.

Then either he would die here or he must leave Belville and find his way to some other village, one where there was still a priest. Did he have the strength for that? And what if the result was just as fruitless as here?

His mind swung desperately from one decision to its opposite, the pain in his head ratcheting up each time.

Life, fate, whatever it was – maybe God, as hollow and heartless as that pile of grey stones – had cheated him. He was broken. Not many hours ago he had gazed down on the world from on high like an Olympian deity. He had done impossible things – his talent, his contribution. But now he might never do them again, he might never again work such wonders. That was over. He was no god. He was barely even a man. Last night he had been reduced to clutching the earth in terror and crawling under hedges and bushes; now look at him, weeping like a child.

A squealing and clanking noise shattered the silence and broke through his thoughts. It was followed by the splash and gush of running water. It was a long time now since his last drink, and the day was hot. How good that flow of water sounded, how good it would be to drink his fill.

The sound was coming from the direction of the cottage behind him. As it stopped, he warily parted the tall blades of grass.

Unlike so much of the rest of the village, this dwelling was undamaged. Its owner had been fortunate. Archie saw things now that he had not noticed earlier, when all his focus was on reaching the church: the whitewashed walls of this cottage were intact, the thatched roof was sound. No broken window panes, no rusting farm equipment in the yard. A small lean-to greenhouse stood at the rear of the cottage, perfectly neat and tidy. There was even a bicycle. Everything looked orderly and cared for.

The back door had been closed when he came to the barn, but now it stood open. As he watched, a young woman came outside and resumed pumping water into a bucket, the task that had caused the noise. She worked smoothly at the pump with fluent strokes, her body leaning into the task, her bare feet planted apart for balance. When she raised her head, he saw that she was perhaps two or three years younger than himself. Her slight build made her seem younger. Her bare arms and legs were lightly tanned, and her auburn hair was cropped short, a practical, no-nonsense cut.

There was an ease in her movements that made him forget his pain. It was the simple beauty of ordinary everyday life. Life without war.

When the bucket was full, she carried it indoors. He caught a glimpse of the fire that was smouldering in the grate despite the heat of the morning. Its embers were low, but as he watched, she bent down and stoked it to life, filled a kettle from the bucket and set it to heat over the flaming logs.

When she was moving about indoors, he could no longer see what she was doing, but after a few minutes she came outside and moved a wooden wringer down the yard in his direction, setting it beside a clothes line that was stretched between two trees.

He realised that she was doing her laundry. Now, when she returned indoors, he was able to imagine her at work, soaking and scrubbing and rinsing. Somehow he knew that all her movements would be as practised and effortless as her work at the pump. He lowered his head to the ground, rested it there, was able to see her in his mind's eye, and allowed himself a brief moment or two of respite from his predicament.

After a time he heard her return to the pump and begin drawing a fresh supply of water. He realised he had been waiting for her. He raised his head and watched her again; he could not help himself. The pain had not diminished, but just the sight of her soothed him. He would have been happy to watch her for the rest of the day – for the rest of his life – this ordinary young girl doing her ordinary work.

But that was not reality. Reality was this damaged and

exhausted body of his, the mortal danger he was in, and the decision that faced him. He was very weak now, weaker than ever, his own fault for letting time slip by, and he knew that another of his blackouts was on the way – he sensed it would be a real blackout this time, not an innocent, recuperative sleep.

And the terrible pain was back, triumphant and crippling. This next blackout might be the one from which he would not return.

God only knew what he thought this young woman could do for him if he did approach her, indeed what anyone could do at this stage, for he might have left it too late; but one way or another he had to make his decision.

There was never any indication that there was anyone but the young woman in the cottage. He had heard no voice from within, she had never spoken to anyone, he saw no one else moving about in the shaded interior.

She returned outside with a copper basin, which he could see was full of wet laundry, and carried it to the clothes line. Here she paused and stared into space for a time, as though lost in some daydream. Then she sighed and got back to work. She began to peg up some items of clothing from the basin. All were feminine garments – dresses, blouses, lingerie and underwear he had no right to be seeing.

It was time; he had to make his decision. There was a loose concrete block at the base of the barn wall, just beside where he lay. He removed the block, worked his maps and the tin box of the escape kit into the gap, and pushed the block back in place. But he kept the .38 revolver in his waistband and the carton of bullets in his pocket.

She was raising the clothes line when he stood up. He

was unsteady, felt himself beginning to sway, but he managed to hold his ground.

She saw him. She stepped back. There was fear in her face, in her eyes. Those eyes, so dark.

He raised his hands in an attempt to reassure her. He stepped closer.

'Aidez-moi,' he said, his voice a dry whisper. 'S'il vous plaît.'

Help me. Please.

Then the world went dark.

Part Two
Engländer

It seemed that Major Friedrich Klemt of the Gestapo was not one for introductions or wasted breath.

'You are relieved of your duties here,' was the entirety of his greeting to Heinrich.

Heinrich blinked. Had he heard right? Perhaps with all the racket in the farmyard, he had misheard what the Gestapo man had said.

'Herr Major? I don't understand.'

But Klemt simply gazed past him into the distance, like a man thinking great thoughts, and added nothing to his statement, offered no explanation. The thin mouth remained firmly shut. It was left to Naumann to explain. His embarrassment was obvious.

'Major Klemt intends to take personal command of the search operation,' he said softly.

Heinrich stared at Naumann. He was being relieved of the search?

His face revealed nothing as he turned to Klemt. 'Herr Major, with respect, there is no need to put yourself to such inconvenience. I acknowledge that I have not yet apprehended the enemy pilot, but I remain confident I can do so. At one point, we almost had him. Furthermore, it's only thanks to me that –'

He got no further. Klemt's head swivelled in its mechanical way. The glacial blue eyes fixed on Heinrich. They were dead eyes, alien behind their blonde lashes.

'You would argue with an order? *My* order?'

'Certainly not, Herr Major. That is not my intention. But surely –'

Naumann lifted a hand to silence Heinrich. He removed his spectacles and pressed the bridge of his nose.

'Heinrich, Major Klemt's decision is no reflection on

you, I assure you. Your conduct of the search has been exemplary.'

'Thank you for saying so, Herr Major. And I hope all other aspects of the performance of my duties have been acceptable.'

'Of course, Heinrich. More than acceptable – everything has been exemplary.'

'Thank you again, Herr Major.'

Naumann's reassurance seemed sincere. Still, something must have transpired between the Wehrmacht major and Klemt before they came out here this morning. It was as though Naumann knew something that he was keeping from Heinrich, something he had not known last night in the Château de Tailleville. Perhaps he was simply unable to share it while the Gestapo officer was present. Or – and this was a worrying thought – he was *unwilling* to share it because he had arrived at some private arrangement with Klemt. An arrangement, perhaps, that left Heinrich high and dry.

They had their understanding, Heinrich and Naumann. It was an understanding that Heinrich nurtured with great care because so much depended on it. It was founded on their common ground as honest Wehrmacht soldiers. Naumann did not want this war or this occupation any more than Heinrich did, but there was no way for either of them to escape. So here they were, stuck far from home in a foreign land where people wanted to kill them, and they looked out for one another, naturally they did – precisely as good Wehrmacht soldiers should. What a dangerous state of affairs it would be if Naumann were to break their understanding now.

'Heinrich?'

He realised that Naumann was addressing him. The

major had put his spectacles on and was watching him closely. Heinrich studied him just as closely in return. Was that sorrow he detected in Naumann's eyes? Perhaps shame as well. Perhaps awareness of letting his best and most trusted officer down was beginning to gnaw at him.

'Heinrich, you are to return to the Kommandantur and await Major Klemt's return.'

And now Klemt himself finally bothered to speak once more, bringing matters to a close with what were clearly his favourite words. His right arm shot out, his heels clicked together.

'Heil Hitler!'

So that was that. End of discussion, such as it had been. Evidently, no more was to be said. Heinrich was being dismissed as if he was of no more significance than the lowliest private soldier. Then again, it was a small price to pay for being done with the search.

He glanced at Klemt, this perfect Aryan and no doubt perfect Nazi, whose gaze remained focused on distant horizons and lofty thoughts inaccessible to ordinary men. His arm was still raised. He did not look happy to be kept waiting – particularly for the second time that morning and by the same two Wehrmacht officers.

Naumann seemed to have come to the same realisation. His arm shot out, his heels clicked.

'Heil Hitler!'

Heinrich sighed quietly to himself. The game had to be played out. No half measures. Regardless of any snubs dealt him by Klemt, Oberleutnant Heinrich Hauser remained a loyal and trustworthy servant of the Reich. Yes, of course he did. And was surely seen to be.

He raised his arm. Raised it high. An arm of steel that would have gladdened his Führer's heart. No feeling sick this time. He would not permit it.

'Heil Hitler!'

The salutation rang out loud and clear and proud, audible even over the noise and bustle in the farmyard. Heads turned.

Heinrich strode across the farmyard to the Kübel, kicked the new tyre to test its roadworthiness – though he would have preferred to be kicking Klemt's bony head – leapt aboard, gunned the engine and was gone without a backward glance.

But not to head to Tailleville. Not to make for the Kommandantur.

Marie gasped as the man collapsed. His legs gave way, he sank to his knees, crumpled to the ground and was lost from view in the tall grass.

She made her way cautiously down the length of the yard, pausing several times as she drew closer to him. He never moved. Could he be dead? Had he just this moment died before her very eyes? Or was it all a trick of some kind?

He had fallen on his back. She went closer. It was not a trick; he lay utterly still, his eyes closed. She pushed through the grass and knelt beside him. She could see now that he was alive, though perhaps only just, for his breathing was shallow, as if each breath might be his last.

What was she to do? He might yet die. But if he did not, and regained consciousness, he could be dangerous.

She should fetch help. She should not try to handle this on her own; she should fetch a neighbour.

But an instinct told her not to do any such thing. Who was to say what kind of danger he might pose? The less that people knew, the better. Belville being Belville, it was possible that someone already knew he was here, had seen him arrive, whoever he was.

She calmed herself and tried to take stock of the situation. The man did not *look* dangerous. He stank and he was a filthy mess, his clothing, face and hands caked with dirt, but she could hardly consider herself endangered by those considerations. Many people fell on hard times these days and took to wandering the countryside in search of food – and sometimes anything they could steal – their clothes becoming more and more ragged, their bodies unwashed and malodorous. As vagabonds and beggars, they were breaking the law – Reich law – but that did not stop them. In desperation, they drifted out from the cities and came even here, to the prohibited coastal zone. Heini bemoaned the fact that he and his comrades were never able to stop all of them.

This man's condition was as bad as that of any vagrant she had ever seen. And he was also injured, which was presumably what had caused his collapse, for she saw now that what she had thought at a distance was some kind of cap or beret on his head was in fact a bandage, blackened by blood and dirt.

So who was he? Where had he come from and why was he here? Why had this nearly dead stranger chosen her land, her property, to drag himself to, like an animal seeking its final resting place?

Whatever the answers, it was not in her nature to ignore the plight of someone in need, stranger though he was. She could not simply leave him with a head injury from which he might die. She would take a chance, she would help him – hoping that he lived – and send him on his way as soon as she possibly could.

Again, she moved closer to him. His lips were dry and cracked, suggesting he was in need of water, so perhaps that was a good place to start. She hurried back to the cottage, fetched a glass tumbler and filled it at the pump. She settled herself in the grass and placed a hand behind his head to raise it from the ground, forcing herself to ignore the revulsion she felt at touching that filthy bandage, and brought the tumbler to his lips and tilted it, hoping he would swallow. At first he choked and coughed the water out, but she persisted, until gradually the water was entering his mouth without being expelled.

As her efforts began to succeed, her confidence grew, and so did her curiosity to know more about him: in fact, to know *something* about him. She studied his face. What was his age? She could not tell; he could be anything from twenty to Heini's age. The stubble on his cheeks was very short, just like Heini's each morning, suggesting he had shaved recently. She examined his hands. They were dirty, but the dirt was not engrained. So he was unlikely to be one of those wandering vagrants she had been thinking about. Nor did he labour for his living; the hands were not calloused. They were not hands that wielded a spade or a scythe or worked the land or handled animals.

Suddenly, he stirred. Her heart thumped. His eyelids quivered, flickered open, then closed briefly and opened again. This time they remained open. She saw that his eyes were a soft shade of hazel, in fact almost golden. She watched as his gaze tried to focus, looking not at her but at the sky. Then he found her face and held her gaze. Her heart thumped again. For a long moment, they regarded one another.

She collected herself and cleared her throat softly.

'Drink,' she told him. 'You need to drink.'

She brought the tumbler to his lips again. He tried to lift his head but seemed to lack the strength to manage by himself, so once again she placed a hand behind his head to help him. He took a sip of water, then another, then took a deeper draught, draining the tumbler.

'Can you stand up?' she asked. 'Try. You must try.'

He pressed his hands flat on the ground and tried to push himself to a sitting position. But he failed and slumped back down with a defeated grunt.

'Again,' she urged. 'I'll help you.'

She put her hands to his back, and this time he rose slowly and with obvious discomfort to a kneeling position. She positioned herself in front of him, grasping his hands so that he could rise to his feet. Her hands seemed like a child's within his hands. Now he was facing her. The hazel eyes gazed at her. Once again, she felt that thump in her heart, like a single drum beat.

He succeeded in getting himself on his feet and fully upright, but at the end of the manoeuvre, he winced, swaying slightly. He was almost a head taller than her; if he lost his balance, she would not be able to keep him from falling.

He muttered something, but she could not make out the words. She frowned, and he realised that she was puzzled.

'My head,' he said. 'My head hurts. Worse when I move.'

This time she understood.

'You're not French?'

He shook his head, which she saw at once was a mistake for him, just as he had said, because pain contorted his features again. But still he offered no clue to his nationality.

If not French, then what? she wondered. Wandering about in this prohibited area and not even French? She felt a stab of anxiety but had no time to deal with it, because at that moment, he swayed again.

'No more talk,' she said – unnecessarily, since he was now so clearly beyond speech.

She lifted his right arm and positioned it across her shoulders, putting both her arms about him to provide additional support. As her arms encircled him, she felt a sharp pain in her ribs. Some hard object was pressing against her. She drew back and searched between their bodies for the cause. Her hand met cold metal – there was a gun in his waistband; it had been hidden by his sweater.

He said nothing, merely repositioned the weapon so that it was no longer pressing into her.

Again, she felt a stab of anxiety. She was used to guns – like many country people, Papa had always owned guns, until the occupation anyway – but why did this man need to be armed? Under Reich law, guns were forbidden to civilians.

She managed to get him all the way up the yard, step by awkward step. The narrowness of the cottage doorway almost defeated them, but somehow she got him through and lowered him down to the couch.

He was bound to be hungry – anyone in his condition would be hungry – but her priority as she saw it was the injury to his head. She had no medical training, but she understood hygiene. And she had soap, thanks to Heini – real soap, not the ersatz substitute that made no lather or crumbled to sticky dust.

She stoked up the fire and set the kettle to boil, just as she had done for her laundry. She peeled off the filthy bandage and put it on the fire, spread towels to protect the couch, and got to work, dabbing gently at his wound with thoroughly soaked cloths that she washed and rinsed frequently. She knew it must be agony for him, but he never complained. Only once did he flinch at her touch, but he assured her he was fine. All he requested was more water to drink. His thirst seemed unquenchable.

Slowly, the wound came clean. When she was satisfied she had done as much as she could, she cut up an old bedsheet and used it as a fresh bandage.

He was lucky, she told him: whatever had caused his injury had ripped out chunks of hair and flesh, but it had not penetrated to the bone of his skull.

'God has been very kind to you.'

The stranger said nothing, just turned his gaze away.

'You don't agree?'

'Thank you for helping me.' He raised his hand to his head and explored the new bandage. 'You're the one who's been kind. Thank you for fixing me up.'

'How did your injury happen? An accident?' She suspected it could be nothing of the sort. Was the gun anything to do with it? What if the injury was in fact a bullet wound?

Again he offered no response.

She shrugged. 'As you wish.'

His French seemed to be as good as Heini's. And from the few words he had uttered, perhaps his accent was similar. So could he be German? In her experience, Germans came with all sorts of accents.

With that thought, she felt the frisson of anxiety again. What if he was a Wehrmacht deserter?

Perhaps it was best not to ask him any more questions. Heinrich was no saint, that was certain, but he was a courageous man who cared about the soldiers under his command and had firm ideas about honour and duty; he would have no sympathy with a deserter. Perhaps it was better for her not to know too much about this man. She had done all she could for him; it was time to send him on his way. And time for her to make sure, as far as she could, that his passing presence here did not attract trouble, not only for her but most of all for Heini.

She went out to the yard and washed her hands at the pump while the man rose from the couch and took a few paces about the room to stretch his legs. When she returned, she was businesslike and brisk. She had rehearsed her words.

'I've done all I can for you, and I think you're fit

enough to leave now,' she said. 'I don't want anyone to see you here on my property, but you can go out to the pump to wash – that's safe enough, no one will see you there – then you can have something to eat. And I'll prepare food that you can take with you. Was it food you came here looking for? Never mind, it doesn't matter – I'll give you some food to take anyway.'

He listened in silence. She realised she was talking too much, more than she had planned and rehearsed, but she could not stop herself.

'You know, I don't really care how you got your injury or who you are or what you're doing here – or what you're running from – but if you're caught with that gun, you'll be in very serious trouble. And I don't want your trouble to involve me. So after you've eaten, you have to be out of here and as far away as possible. And you must never tell anyone you were here or that I helped you. Do you understand? I don't want any trouble.'

As she spoke, she busied herself fetching bread, cheese and ham, and began setting a place at the table for him in the small kitchen area of the cottage. But despite her determination to stick to practicalities, her mind was elsewhere.

It was not only anxiety that was making her prattle. She was aware of those hazel eyes watching her as she went from larder to table and back again. She was aware of his gaze following her every move. As if he was hungering for more than food.

Archie went out to the pump as she had commanded. He was in a daze but not only because of his exhaustion and injury. Never in his life had he felt so bewildered; never had his emotions been in such turmoil.

The reason was simple. He was in love with this woman.

In love. Words that he heard in every popular song of the day, words that as a consequence had long ago lost their actual meaning for him and had become trite and empty – until now, this hardest and longest night and day of his life, when their power had come thundering over him.

How could this happen? It was madness. Yet he was as certain of his feelings as he was of the sun above or the moon that had brought him to this woman's country. And his feelings were more than physical attraction alone. He knew that too. He desired her with a fierceness he had never felt before for any woman, and he knew well enough how his body had responded to her beauty and her close physical presence. But he also knew that his feelings for her were more than that. He had been in love with her since his first glimpse of her working in this yard, absorbed by her task and entirely unaware of his presence. A case of love at first sight. When he came back to consciousness after his collapse, she was the first thing he saw, a wonderful mirage and no longer distant but right there before him, so close to him that he could feel her breath on his face and taste its sweetness. It was as if those dark eyes held his destiny, as if all of his life had been leading to that moment.

As to whether she felt anything for him, of course he could not possibly hope for that. And even if she did, what would be the use? How could love ever come to anything under these circumstances of war and occupation? To think in terms of destiny was foolish. This was chance, not destiny. A chance encounter that was coming to an end, as she had made perfectly clear with her laboured instructions to him to be on his way.

But that was not all. There was yet more to his quandary. Perhaps the wound to his head had stopped him thinking straight, for there was in fact real danger here for him, and he would do well to acknowledge that. He had put himself in this woman's hands, but who was she? *What* was she?

While she was tending to his wound, he had glanced around the room, looking for clues about her. He saw some books, a few framed snapshots – one of an elderly man and woman who might have been her parents, another of a child who was a younger version of herself. But his gaze had also fallen on some items by the hearth: an ashtray, a pack of cigarettes, a small box of matches. At the sight of them, a jolt of fear had shot through him, so powerful that she felt him flinch. She had apologised, thinking she had hurt him.

Cigarettes and matches. Ordinary possessions, to be found in any home – except for the fact that this particular matchbox bore the black emblem of the German imperial eagle, and the cigarettes were Reemtsma, a German brand.

Later, when she went outside and he stood up and walked about the room to stretch his legs, he crossed to the hearth to confirm what he had seen. There was no mistake.

Why did she have German cigarettes and matches? Were they hers? How did they come to be here? Perhaps they belonged to a visitor. If that was the case, that person was apparently a frequent caller, one who presumed to leave their cigarettes here in anticipation of their next visit.

Or did their owner actually reside here with her? A male owner, perhaps. Those garments she had been pegging on the clothes line – all of them were feminine. No evidence there of a male presence, just as he could detect none in the cottage itself. But that was hardly definitive proof. It merely brought him to another puzzle. He was no expert in female attire, but it seemed to him that the delicate garments she was laundering must be costly and available only to the fortunate and favoured few. How could this seemingly ordinary young woman afford such luxuries? Were they gifts? If so, from whom? How did she merit them?

He faced the question squarely. Was she a collaborator? Had he lost his heart to a collaborator? Was he that much of a fool? Had he bungled things so badly that he had ended up with precisely the result he had tried so hard to avoid – had he put himself in the hands of someone who would betray him?

Was there a telephone in this cottage? Having fooled him into thinking he was safe, she could be calling her German masters right now to report his presence.

Then he saw her. She was not making a telephone call – if she even had a telephone. She was standing at the table, wrapping food in a cloth for him to take with him when he left, exactly as she had promised.

He felt stupid and ungrateful, ashamed of his suspicions. She had not merely taken care of him; she had probably saved his life, even risking her own life in doing so. And there she was now, arranging to put food in his undeserving belly. Yet this was how he responded to her kindness, indeed to her courage – with suspicion and distrust. There could be plenty of innocent ways to explain the anomalies that troubled him.

At that moment, she raised her head and glanced out at him. He leaned on the pump handle – certainly less expertly than she would have done – and drew more water. He would have had to strip completely to do a thorough job of washing himself, and that was out of the question, so he was using the flow of the water to rinse and scrub the worst of the dirt from his clothes. The ancient pump was noisy, even when she used it, and was all the more so in his inexpert hands. Each time he worked the handle, the clank and squeal of the mechanism and the gush of the water obliterated all other sounds.

But this time, as the water stopped flowing and its noise abated, he heard the sound of a vehicle door slamming shut somewhere nearby. He felt a sudden rush of fear. Someone had arrived at the cottage, the approach of their vehicle unheard by him. And he had a feeling it was unlikely to be a civilian vehicle.

Now a voice called out. A man's voice.

'Marie! Where are you, Marie?'

As she looked out from the shaded interior of the cottage, her eyes grew wide in alarm, but she continued to hold Archie's gaze.

And he knew her name now.

Once again, Heinrich had thrashed the little Kübelwagen along Normandy's narrow roads and lanes, this time from the search zone back to Belville. There was a great deal to do and, he suspected, little time in which to do it. This time, there had been no comradely chats with the troopers manning the checkpoints or out on patrol. No jokes, no wisecracks.

'You've received new orders?' he demanded brusquely each time he was flagged down. His face was stern. 'You've been briefed to be on the lookout for a fugitive?'

The troopers read his mood with accuracy. They were equally curt in response.

'Yes, Herr Oberleutnant. A foreign spy, we're told. We are alert.'

The barrier was lifted; off he went.

On arrival at Marie's cottage, he made straight for the yard. He knew his sweet Marie. On a fine day like this, that was where he would find her – not lazing in the hot sun, for she was too conscientious for that, but keeping up with outdoor tasks: her laundry, perhaps, or in her greenhouse, tending to her little vegetable garden, or in the barn, where she stored her potatoes and root vegetables.

His heart turned over to think of her going about her day, untroubled. Was she missing him? He yearned to see her, to hold her in his arms, to console himself with her love.

Why was the Gestapo man here? Why did he want Heinrich to return to the Kommandantur and wait for him there? Why could he not deal with what was on his mind right there and then at the search zone? These Gestapo types always had to be devious.

Whichever way Heinrich tried to analyse the situation,

always he came back to the question of what Klemt was after. It might be true that he had a particular interest in Resistance operations. It might be true that he was just the man to pursue enemies of the Reich, those troublesome and stubborn French citizens who kept getting in the way of the Reich's plans. But what if he poked his bony Aryan nose into places that were best left alone? What if his investigations led him to stumble upon other matters? Matters such as Heinrich's business activities. If that happened, the danger was that he would not stop there. Everything else could be in jeopardy as well.

Everything else?

Yes, everything. It could all unravel, including matters that Heinrich hardly dared allow himself to think about. The deepest secrets of all. *His* deepest secrets.

Thus was he fretting as he rounded the corner into Marie's yard, calling her name.

And saw the man.

He knew at once who he was, who he had to be. And he knew that a bad situation had just become immeasurably worse. This was the Lysander pilot, the very man he had spent the night looking for, the man he had not wanted to find. The subject of the search from which, to his relief, he had just been removed. And here he was, in Marie's yard.

The man was standing by the water pump. He did not seem to be armed. He was young, not much older than Marie. Water dripped from his clothing and face. A white bandage encircled his head. Perhaps the bullet fired beside the potato field had found its mark after all.

He stared at Heinrich, evidently just as surprised as Heinrich himself.

It was Heinrich who broke the spell. He had no idea how the situation might develop; he knew only that he had to take control of it, just as he had taken control of the search for this man. In one movement, his Luger pistol was out of its holster and grasped in both hands as he raised it to eye level and stepped forward. The man did not move but stood there dripping water.

'Heini!'

Marie had appeared in the doorway, halted in her rush towards him, her eyes wide with fear as she stared at the pistol.

Heinrich felt relief flood through him. She was safe. On that at least, his mind could be at rest.

'Has he hurt you, Marie?'

'No, Heinrich, of course not. Why would he hurt me after what I've done for him?'

After what I've done for him. What did she mean by that?

'Down on the ground,' he told the man, in German.

The man did not move. He had not understood. Heinrich repeated the command in French and gestured with the Luger.

The man went down on his knees.

Marie was still standing in the doorway.

'Go back indoors, meine Liebe.'

She obeyed. Heinrich returned his attention to his captive.

'All the way down, Engländer. That's who you are, isn't it? You're the Engländer, the pilot. So now we meet.'

The Engländer said nothing, but stretched his arms out and lowered himself to the ground until he was flat on his stomach.

'Very good. Now don't move.'

Heinrich placed a foot on his back to pin him down and yanked the bandage from his head, exposing the raw wound beneath it. He could see it had been carefully cleaned.

He forced the man's arms behind his back and used the bandage to bind his wrists tightly together. As he tugged the knot tight, he spotted the revolver in the Engländer's waistband. An armed man, an enemy pilot, on the run in German territory, no doubt desperate: and alone here with Marie. God in heaven, anything could have happened. It did not bear thinking about.

He took the revolver and checked the safety before securing the weapon in his own belt. As he went through the Engländer's pockets, he found a small carton of bullets. He took it.

Leaving the man tethered and prostrate by the pump, he called for Marie and led her down the yard, out of earshot of the man but where he could keep a close eye on him.

She was trembling, badly shaken by what had happened.

'You're angry, Heini. Have I done something wrong?'

'No, I'm not angry,' he told her truthfully. 'I'm just relieved you're safe. But what exactly did you do for this man?' He spoke gently, for he could see how frightened she was. 'Don't be afraid, I'm not going to be cross. Tell me everything. What did you do for him?'

Her words came tumbling out in a nervous rush. 'I saw to his injury, that wound on his head. I cleaned it and bandaged it. He could have caught an infection otherwise. He might have died. How could I let that happen? You know I could never do that, Heini, not with anyone, stranger or not.'

'I understand, meine Liebe. Has he been in your cottage?'

'I had to take him inside to wash the wound properly.'

His heart sank. Sweet, kind Marie.

'Did you know he had a gun?'

'Yes, I saw it.'

'Did he threaten you with it?'

'I saw the gun, but he never threatened me. No.'

'Did he force you to help him?'

'No, Heinrich, never.'

'So you treated his wound. And what else happened between you?'

'*Between* us? Nothing happened *between* us! Just before you arrived, I told him he had to leave. I said he had to go as soon as he finished washing. I said I didn't want him to be seen here, on my property. No one must know he was here. I prepared food for him. I said he mustn't involve me if he got caught with that gun.'

Heinrich's heart sank further. Every word she spoke was her death sentence. It would be his as well. She did not see that, of course. She was as innocent as a child. She *was* a child. A child who meant well, a child overflowing with good deeds.

'Do you know who he is, Heini? I thought he might be German, a deserter, but maybe not, because I don't think he understood when you spoke to him in German.'

He sighed. 'I do know who he is. He's a wanted man but not a deserter. He's not German. I've been searching for him all night. The whole garrison has been out looking for this man.'

At this, she became even more distraught. 'Does he have anything to do with the explosion last night?'

'He has everything to do with it. He's an English pilot.

He brings foreign agents and spies to France. He was on a mission when his aircraft crashed. He's not in uniform, so that makes him a spy too. You've helped an English spy.'

The colour drained from her face. If there had been conversation of any kind between her and the Engländer, clearly she had remained oblivious to the truth.

But as innocent as she was, she now had to appreciate the gravity of the situation, even if she could not be told all its aspects. He put his arms about her and gently kissed her forehead. The situation was a catastrophe, and there was only one way out of it that he could see.

'Listen carefully, meine Liebe. This is very important. A Gestapo officer has come from Caen. I may be in danger from him. That's why I'm here now – I need to make certain precautionary arrangements. But now you're in danger as well – because of this Engländer, because you helped him. If the Gestapo officer finds out what you did, he'll arrest you for protecting and sheltering an enemy of the Reich. Only one punishment is possible.'

'But I didn't know –'

'Of course not, but this Gestapo officer won't care. All he'll care about is the fact that you didn't report the spy, you helped him of your own free will and not at gunpoint, you saved his life, you took him into your home and gave him food, you knew he was armed, you told him to stay out of sight, you warned him he was in danger. The list goes on. These are all serious crimes, and all of this will come out.'

'No! I don't have to tell the Gestapo officer any of that. I won't tell him, you won't tell him. And if we don't tell him, how can he know?'

'Because he'll interrogate us. He'll use torture. That's

what the Gestapo do.' He turned to look back up the yard at the Engländer. 'And anyway, what you or I tell him is neither here nor there.'

'What do you mean?'

Heinrich took a breath. He hated what he was about to do. What he *had* to do. Never once in their relationship had he sought to manipulate Marie or take advantage of her trusting nature. But in this instance, he had no choice.

'Marie, the man is an enemy of the Reich. I have to hand him over, I have to turn him in. That's a problem because *he* will be the one who'll tell everything you did. He too will be interrogated, you see. You and I will be arrested. And executed – both of us, because I'll be considered as guilty as you.' He paused to let that sink in. 'There's only one way to prevent all this happening. The Engländer has to die. I have to kill him.'

She made a small whimper of protest. Her hand flew to her mouth.

'No, Heinrich! You can't possibly do that!'

'I'll say he put up a struggle, he was armed and I had to shoot him. His gun will be proof.'

'No, Heini! Please!'

'We have to be realistic. He'll be executed anyway, as an enemy spy. There's no alternative. I can't just let him go free. Sooner or later, he'd be captured and we'd be back where we started.'

'But why does your Gestapo officer have to know we have this man? He doesn't know he's here – and he doesn't *have* to know. If he doesn't know that, then he won't find out anything else.'

'That's impossible. Of course he has to know. I have to tell him.'

'But why?' She pressed herself closer, placed her

hands on his chest and gazed up at him.

Her gentle touch, her soft body pressing against him: these joys were exactly what he had been longing for. But not these circumstances.

Her eyes pleaded. 'We can hide the man, Heini. Yes, we can, and you know exactly where and how, the same as I do. Then we'll be safe. Please, Heini, we must hide him. Do this for me.'

'I don't know. You know I'd do anything for you, meine Liebe. But what you're asking . . .'

'Do this one thing for me, Heini.'

He made her wait. He closed his eyes for a long moment, then finally nodded.

She was overjoyed. She stretched up on tiptoe and pressed her lips on his.

It was done. It gave him no satisfaction, but it was done.

Sweet Marie, who would never hurt a fly. In her thinking, it would always be her idea, not his. She would have no reason ever to wonder why her Heini, a loyal Wehrmacht officer through and through, wanted to hide and protect an English spy.

Nor would Belville. That was what this was really about. Because everything Marie knew, Belville would come to know.

He kissed her forehead again, tasting the salt in the perspiration that her fear had produced.

'So let us get to work, meine Liebe. Let us hide this young Engländer if that's what you want.'

Flat on the wet ground by the pump, Archie watched Marie and the German as they whispered together. He saw their embraces. Hardest thing of all for him to witness, he saw the loving kiss that Marie bestowed on the German.

To his astonishment, the German untied him and allowed him to stand up. But not in order to release him from captivity. Nor to shoot him there and then, a fate that would have come as no surprise to him. Either that or to be taken away for interrogation and whatever might then follow – which probably meant being shot. Hardly an attractive range of options.

Instead of any of this, the German had other ideas.

'You have work to do, Engländer.' The barrel of the Luger dug into Archie's side as a gentle reminder of its abiding presence. 'And don't get any stupid ideas.'

The German lit a cigarette. Archie saw the brand: Reemtsma. So now he knew who owned the cigarettes and matches on Marie's hearth. That and Marie's kiss removed all doubt as to their relationship.

The German reflected for a moment as he smoked. 'You were clever last night – what you did with the dead man to make us think he was the pilot.' He glanced down at Archie's feet, at his flying boots, and smiled. 'You fooled my comrades. You almost fooled me – almost but not quite. We almost met during the search, we almost came face to face – in that lane, remember? You weren't so clever then – though you did an impressive disappearing act afterwards. One way and another, you gave me a very difficult night.'

Archie gestured towards his wounded head. 'It wasn't exactly easy for me, either.'

'Ach, these things happen. A blunder in the excitement

of the moment. My men were under orders not to shoot.'

'You wanted me alive.'

'Of course. But that doesn't mean I won't shoot you now if I have to. But tell me – your mission last night, what you were doing, you've done it before, yes? You've flown into France before? A dangerous thing to do, I think.'

Archie said nothing.

The German gave a wry smile. 'Don't worry, Engländer, I'm not going to interrogate you. Name, rank, number – all that nonsense is of no interest to me. I'm just curious, that's all. As one soldier to another. But never mind – as I said, there's work to do and no time to waste.'

He took Archie at gunpoint to one of the cottage's two small bedrooms. There was barely room for the door to swing open. The simple bed had been upended and pushed to the wall beside an old oak armoire.

Archie found himself in an Aladdin's cave of what were obviously contraband or stolen goods: wooden cases of wine, of champagne and Armagnac and other spirits; perfumes and cosmetics still in the manufacturers' bulk cartons; German cigarettes including Reemtsma; chocolate; tinned foodstuffs; nylon stockings and expensive lingerie like the garments Marie had been laundering that morning.

It turned out that Archie's work, under his captor's supervision, was to carry all these goods to the graveyard beside the abandoned church. Slave labour, pure and simple, labour for a task that the German would presumably have had to do for himself, perhaps with Marie's help. And a task that was concealed from prying eyes – a gate in the graveyard's perimeter wall where it bordered Marie's land meant that Archie and the German could move between Marie's cottage and the graveyard without being seen from any of the other cottages in the village.

Archie had been vaguely aware of the graveyard when he arrived at the church today but had paid it no particular attention. Now he saw that it was in as bad a state as the church and the ruined cottages. Whatever event had struck them had blighted it as well. It was little better than a wasteland. Many of the graves looked as if they had been torn apart; headstones were broken and leaning at all angles. Efforts had been made to remedy the damage, but the result was still a mess. Weeds and grass sprouted in the gravel paths; uncleared dead leaves were turning to compost in which nettles and thistles thrived.

An ancient yew tree of massive girth, gnarled and ingrown upon itself, watched over the place's slow decay – a tree of the dead in its every twisted bough – but it had somehow escaped whatever disaster had befallen its surroundings. Its survival only heightened the atmosphere of hopelessness and abandonment.

In the furthest corner stood extravagant family mausoleums, hideous edifices to Archie's eyes, surmounted by crucifixes and trumpeting angels. They suggested a time when the village had housed families of wealth. Many of these large tombs had been destroyed, but some had survived, though nature was fast reclaiming them: ivy and bindweed crept over them in profusion.

One of the tombs was almost completely buried beneath shattered chunks of statuary, giving the impression that it had collapsed on itself. In fact, beneath the debris and bindweed, it was intact. The German had keys to its bronze door, which he unlocked so that Archie could add his loads to the quantities of goods that were already stockpiled within. The place was huge, intended for many generations that had never arrived. It was grisly work there in the gloom among the rows of stacked burial caskets. Archie realised that the place was in effect the German's warehouse – long-term storage that was dry and safe, cool in summer and protected from winter frost. The stocks held in the cottage were probably to enable day-to-day trading.

He wondered who the customers were. He knew the reputation that the occupying Germans had earned for themselves as looters who were plundering France; now he was seeing this for himself, for there was plenty of evidence here. He wondered if some of the goods also found their way into unscrupulous French hands. Did black markets take sides? He suspected not.

But why clear everything out of the cottage? Sharp businessman that the German evidently was, he was sure to have a good reason.

And however hard Archie worked, it was never fast enough for him. The German seemed anxious to be gone, as though he had urgent business elsewhere. It was only thanks to Marie that Archie was allowed to eat and rest.

'Remember his injury, Heinrich.'

He was grateful for her intervention. Meanwhile he had learned another name, that of his German captor.

He still expected to be shot. The work would be only a temporary reprieve. He doubted that Marie could prevent what was to happen. He had no reason to suppose she would even try – after all, she had done nothing to protect him when the German had taken him prisoner and disarmed him. And he realised now that he would not be taken into official custody – the German was operating on the wrong side of Reich law and Archie knew too much. Once today's work was done, his eventual fate was certain: he would have to be shot.

In which case the madness of falling in love with Marie was the least of his worries.

Unless he could outsmart the German, this Heinrich.

So throughout every minute of the work, with every crossing that he made from cottage to graveyard and back again, Archie looked for his opportunity, his chance to overpower Heinrich somehow, grab the Luger from him – possibly retrieve his own revolver as well – and escape. If he died in the attempt, he would be no worse off. He steeled himself for action – even though he was not entirely sure what that action might be.

But the German never lowered his guard, the Luger never wavered, and the .38 revolver remained firmly out of Archie's reach.

At last Archie fetched the final case of champagne from the cottage and carried it into the tomb.

It was now or never. Instead of setting the heavy case down on the flagstone floor, he spun around and used his momentum to fling the case at the German. But he was not fast enough. He could blame his weakened physical condition. Or even his emotional state. Or the fact that he had left it too late. He could blame Heinrich for working him to the point of exhaustion. He could make all the excuses he wished, but the result was the same: the German had read his intentions and was ready for him. He stepped neatly out of the way, the wooden case crashed harmlessly to the floor, and Archie felt his head explode in an overwhelming burst of pain. In his final moment of consciousness, he realised that Heinrich had clubbed him with the Luger.

The daylight vanished. The bronze door clanged shut. Then came the sound of keys turning in the lock, followed by the crunch of boots on gravel as the German strode off.

Then silence. Darkness and silence. And blessed unconsciousness.

Heinrich reached the Kommandantur just in time, for Naumann and Klemt arrived only a few minutes after him, finding him waiting in Naumann's outer office.

As they entered, Heinrich jumped to his feet, the model of a good Wehrmacht soldier, and delivered a brisk salute. A conventional Wehrmacht salute this time. Klemt ignored him, offering no salute of any kind.

Heinrich addressed Naumann. 'Herr Major, if I may enquire, has the enemy pilot been found?'

Naumann's gaze slid briefly to Klemt as he shook his head. It was a carefully minimal, discreet shake. It would not do to announce failure too boldly, he was signalling, not when the failure had been under the Gestapo man's personal leadership of the search.

'The search has been called off, Heinrich.'

Heinrich felt a weight lift from his shoulders. He faced Klemt.

'Then what is your plan now, Herr Major?'

Klemt showed no sign of having heard him.

'Take this man's sidearm,' he ordered Naumann. 'Then show us to an interview room. Post an armed guard – but outside the room, not inside. Proceedings at this stage will be confidential.'

Heinrich stood at attention in the interview room while Klemt settled his meagre frame in the comfortably padded chair at the table that was the only other piece of furniture. He removed his cap and placed it carefully on the table, passing his hand over his cropped blond hair as if making sure it was tidy. It was too short *not* to be tidy.

He had brought nothing with him to the room – no briefcase, no paperwork.

'This is a preliminary and informal discussion,' he

said, sitting back and crossing his legs. 'Should a formal discussion prove necessary, a formal record will then be kept. Do you understand?'

'Yes, Herr Major.'

'State your name and rank.'

Heinrich obliged.

'Certain allegations have been made against you. Are you aware of them?'

Heinrich gazed at the wall. 'No, Herr Major. What are these allegations?'

'You're not permitted to know.'

'I see. Then perhaps I may ask who has made these allegations.'

'You're not permitted to know.'

'Herr Major, how can I defend myself if I don't know what I'm accused of?'

'Why do you assume you must defend yourself? What is it you think you must defend yourself against? An innocent man has no need to defend himself. His innocence is self-evident.'

'With respect, Herr Major, he must defend himself if false allegations are made against him. Even an innocent man must be prepared to do that.'

'So you think these allegations are false?'

'I'm certain of that.'

'How can you be certain without knowing what they are? How can that be?'

'Because it's irrelevant what they are. I haven't done anything wrong, so it follows that they must therefore be false.'

'Yet a minute ago you wanted to know what they were. You contradict yourself. However, I agree with you – if you're innocent, it doesn't matter. But if you were to insist on knowing what the allegations are, I would have to conclude that you must be guilty of something and you want to know whether the allegations relate to that. You might be innocent of the matter or matters to which the allegations relate, while being guilty of some other misdemeanour. Are we agreed?'

Heinrich glanced at him, then returned his gaze to the wall. So this was the expert interrogator at work.

'Herr Major, permit me to make my position clear. First, I'm innocent of any wrongdoing, of any misdemeanour at all. Second, if there are allegations to the contrary, they are completely false. I respectfully suggest that this discussion can therefore be ended.'

Klemt was not interested. The cold eyes remained locked on Heinrich, who now sensed that an important point was coming.

'Have you ever supplied illicit goods – contraband or luxury goods – to any member of the German Military Administration in France, at any location, and to individuals of whatever rank, or to any member of the Reich's fighting or occupation forces in France, also at any location and of whatever rank?'

And there it was, just as Heinrich had feared: the renowned scourge of Resistance criminals also wanted to hunt down stolen bottles of wine. Who could say where else he might want to poke that bony nose?

'Herr Major, I have never supplied such goods to anyone. I would never allow myself to become involved in anything like that.'

'Have you ever supplied such goods to Major Gerhard Naumann?'

'Never, Herr Major. Absolutely not. As I said, I have never supplied such goods to anyone.'

'Are you at present or have you ever been in an intimate relationship with a French civilian?'

'With respect, Herr Major, that is not an offence.'

'You will answer the question.'

'Yes, Herr Major.'

'Yes what? Yes, you agree to answer the question or yes, you are at present or have been in such a relationship?'

'Both, Herr Major.'

For the first time, Klemt showed a flicker of irritation. 'You will be specific.'

'Yes, Herr Major. Yes, I will answer the question. Yes, I am at present in a relationship with a French female.'

The thin lips stretched into a humourless smile. 'So. Now we make progress.'

'What progress is that, Herr Major, since there has been no offence?'

'Are you living with this woman in her home?'

'No, Herr Major.'

'Do you sometimes spend the night in her home when you should be in barracks with your men?'

'No, Herr Major.'

Heinrich could almost see the cogs spinning in the Gestapo man's brain. He was clearly in possession of information with which Heinrich's answer was at odds.

Klemt tried again. 'But you do spend nights with this woman. In her home.'

'Yes, Herr Major. But only when there is no requirement for me to be in barracks.'

Klemt looked triumphant, even though it was Heinrich himself who had tossed him the bone he now seized upon so eagerly.

'And who decides that? Who decides when you should

be in barracks?'

'The duty roster makes it clear.'

'The roster does not take account of unexpected events. It does not take account of emergencies. Last night, for example, you were not in barracks. There was an emergency – the enemy aircraft – but you were not here.'

Heinrich gazed steadily at the wall, careful to show no emotion. But he now knew that Klemt's informant – for he had to have one – was someone who was in a position to know that Heinrich was absent from barracks last night.

'Herr Major, it is true that I was not in barracks. But that did not impair my execution of my duties in any way. Major Naumann can confirm that I was present here in good time when he needed me – *before* he needed me, as it happened. In regard to my duties overall, you heard Major Naumann describe my performance of them as exemplary. Indeed, last night is a good example. As I tried to explain earlier, it was I who detected that the body found beside the enemy aircraft was not its pilot but a decoy intended to deceive us so that we wouldn't search. It was I who saw through that ruse, it was I who deduced that the pilot had survived and was on the run, and it was my initiative to mount the search for him.'

'All very laudable. Yet you failed to capture him.'

'As did you, Herr Major. With respect.'

Klemt actually twitched. The blow had struck home. Heinrich knew it might cost him dearly, but it would be worth it for the pleasure of seeing this perfect Nazi's self-regard punctured, however briefly. It was a sight Heinrich would remember and savour.

Possibly in a prison cell.

Possibly while being led before a firing squad.

The thin smile flitted across Klemt's mouth again. Perhaps he too was thinking about prison cells and firing squads.

'This French whore of yours –'

'She's no whore, Herr Major, I assure you. With respect.'

'Thoughtless of me. But an easy mistake to make, since so many of these French women are exactly that. However, I'm sure you're right. I'll take your word on the matter – there are always honourable exceptions, and I'm sure this French lover of yours is very honourable. May I know her name?'

'Marie.'

'A pretty name. Where does she live?'

'In a small village not far from here.'

'It has a name, this village?'

'Belville.'

'Also a pretty name. So. You will take me to Belville. You will take me to meet Marie.'

Until now, Archie had thought he knew what pain was. But now, as he regained consciousness, he truly discovered its debilitating effect. The slightest move made his head explode all over again.

Memory returned, and with it the realisation that at least he was alive. He had not been shot as he had expected to be. For some reason, the German, Heinrich, had spared him.

He rose unsteadily to his feet and squinted into the darkness around him, searching for any chink of light. He found none, not a glimmer; the tomb, appropriately, was as dark as death itself.

He wondered if it was airtight as well. He hoped not – how long might he be imprisoned here? He belonged in open skies, not in this confined nothingness. He felt the first stirrings of claustrophobia. Was this where he would die? Not in those open skies that he loved, not even pinned to the earth or hunted down as he had feared last night, but in this place of utter blackness.

He was rescued from his bleak speculation by three distinct metallic knocks that echoed in the dark cavern. He turned gratefully towards the sound. Without it, he would not have known where the door was – no light seeped in around its edges. He waited, unwilling to respond until he knew who was there, outside – an irrational precaution, since there was nothing he could do, whoever it was.

The knocks were repeated. This time a voice followed them, only just audible through the thick bronze. To his relief, it was Marie's voice.

'Can you hear me?' she called. 'Are you all right?'

He inched his way cautiously towards the door. As well as burial caskets, there were cases of wine and champagne on the floor, but he could not see them. Despite his care, he barged into one – he suspected it was the one with which he had tried to attack Heinrich – and a fresh bolt of pain shot through his head. He had to stand motionless until it eased.

She knocked again.

'Yes, Marie, I hear you.'

His words caused yet more pain, this time from the reverberation of his voice in his head.

'Ah, good – you're conscious,' she said. 'And you know my name!' She sounded pleased at the discovery.

'Mine is Archie. Can you let me out now?'

'I'm sorry, Archie, I can't do that, because I don't have the keys. Heinrich keeps the keys. But this is the safest place for you.'

'Why do I have to be locked up like this?'

He winced. Every word was agony.

'Heini thinks people may come to search my home. They won't be looking for you, but it's important that you stay out of sight. Heini told me who you are – and what you are – and they'll certainly want to capture you if they find you. It was my idea to hide you here. This tomb is the very best place, I promise you – it's so overgrown and covered with rubble that no one would ever think of breaking it open to look inside. They won't know we have keys for it.'

He considered himself to be imprisoned, but she called it hiding him. And he wondered exactly what Heinrich, this Heini of hers, had told her about him. The truth? In which case, here she was, safe with her German lover and under his protection, yet not only had she taken the risk of helping Archie, tending to his injury, but now she was taking the even greater risk entailed in hiding him – in full knowledge of what he was. And apparently, she was doing so with the approval of the same Heinrich. Surely this meant that the German was also running the same risk.

Why would a German officer do that? It made no sense.

'These people, Marie, the ones who might search your home – did Heinrich say who they are?'

'Of course. They're Germans, like him – Wehrmacht. But they'll be under the command of a Gestapo officer. A very important man, Heini says. Heini doesn't like him. He thinks this Gestapo man will make trouble for him.'

Archie stared into the darkness. It was like staring into his own dark future. Gestapo. A Gestapo officer on his way here while he was trapped and helpless in this tomb. A few moments ago, his poor head with its murderous pain was his biggest concern. Now he had more than a broken head to worry about. A Gestapo officer coming to search for something – presumably stolen contraband goods, the very things with which he was surrounded: he could hardly have got himself in a worse fix. And now the mystery of Marie's Heinrich was deepening even further with her disclosure that the Gestapo officer was after her German lover. Little wonder all those cases of champagne and wine and luxury goods had to be relocated. Little wonder Heinrich had been in such a hurry.

'Will these people be coming today, Marie?'

'I don't know.'

'Well, what does Heinrich think?'

'He doesn't know for sure. Probably today, he thinks, but he says you can never be sure with these important people, these Gestapo.'

'What if it's not today and I have to stay in here and you can't let me out? How long can I stay in here? How long can I survive? What if I run out of air?'

'You won't. There's a gap at the very back. You can't see it because of the way the stone slabs overlap. Light doesn't get in but air does.'

'Are you sure? How can you know that?'

'Don't worry, Archie. Really. When I was a little girl, I used to play with my friends in these old tombs. My father was church sexton. He forbade it, but I did it anyway. This tomb was always the best one for air.'

'Did you know Heinrich was going to crack me on the head?'

'Of course not! He only told me afterwards. I have to go now, Archie. If you open the last case of champagne you brought here, you'll find some food and water I put in there for you. If the Gestapo officer comes and you hear voices outside, just keep very still and quiet – like I used to do as a child. They'll never know you're here, I promise you.'

He was paying dearly for this conversation – every word was a sledgehammer blow inside his head.

'If Heinrich has the keys to this place, how will you be able to let me out when it's safe?'

But he received no answer. She was gone. All he was left with was the darkness. And the echo of his name on her lips.

Heinrich led the way to Belville. He was allowed to drive himself in the Kübelwagen. There was not even an armed guard with him in the vehicle, but he knew better than to interpret this as laxity or any indication of goodwill on Klemt's part. After all, where could he possibly escape to?

Technically speaking, he was not under arrest. He had not had any charges laid against him, only that vague reference to allegations. But he was in custody as assuredly as if he had been shackled hand and foot.

Klemt had refused his request for the return of his Luger.

'But Herr Major, we might come under attack. May I respectfully remind you that the enemy pilot is still at large, since you abandoned the search?'

Klemt was scornful. 'Are you suggesting we should tremble in our boots for fear of one enemy airman? And are you criticising my decision to call off the search? The man is probably dead by now.'

'I bow to your wise judgement, Herr Major. Probably dead, indeed.'

And so they set off, Klemt following behind the Kübel in the Mercedes. Then came an open-backed truck with four armed troopers aboard, completing the convoy.

On the roads, the Wehrmacht units who manned the checkpoints and mobile patrols were on their sharpest behaviour. Evidently, they had been warned by radio of the convoy's approach – and no doubt of the presence of a Gestapo officer. Identity papers were examined scrupulously, even Klemt's – in fact, particularly Klemt's, noted Heinrich approvingly. Clever troopers, to show how keenly they were up to the mark.

For their sake, he did not engage with them, did

nothing that could compromise them or confuse them, did not strike up any friendly banter and allowed himself only a formal nod when they returned his own papers to him. They met his gaze levelly, their response as restrained as his. Restrained and all the more eloquent for being so.

'They know I'm in trouble,' he reflected sadly. 'Ach, the very birds in the sky know.'

The question was, how much trouble? Trouble over a few bottles of wine? Or something more?

He was beginning to suspect that Naumann was in trouble too. Nothing had been said to that effect by either Klemt or Naumann himself, but the Wehrmacht major had been obliged to remain behind in the Kommandantur, on Klemt's direct orders.

'This is my investigation, not yours,' Klemt had told him bluntly. 'Your attendance is unnecessary.'

Heinrich found himself having to revise his earlier views on Naumann. He had thought the major was siding with Klemt, betraying the trust that he and Heinrich had always shared. But now he was beginning to think that Naumann was as much a target of Klemt's investigation as himself – whatever the purpose of that investigation actually was. The Gestapo man's very specific question about whether Naumann had been supplied with illicit goods made that clear. Why single out Naumann without naming any other senior Wehrmacht officer?

There was never any love lost between the Gestapo and the regular soldiers of the Wehrmacht. In all probability, Klemt had been planning his visit to Tailleville and Naumann's Kommandantur for some time, quietly amassing intelligence from whatever informant he had. That was how the Gestapo went about their dirty work. The crash of the Engländer's aircraft had provided a perfect pretext for him to swoop while Heinrich and Naumann were distracted by that event. By keeping them apart, he had made sure they could not confer – that was his real reason for taking over the search, keeping Naumann with him and sending Heinrich back to the Kommandantur to await his return there. As far as Heinrich could see, this led to one conclusion and one conclusion alone: Klemt had no real interest in the search for the Engländer. An expert in partisan and Resistance operations he might be, but that was not why he was here.

So whatever he was really up to, who was his informant? It had to be someone who was aware of Heinrich's regular overnight absences from barracks. Someone interested enough to keep an eye on him. Someone who knew he had been absent from barracks last night. Someone with a powerful motive for getting him out of the way for good.

Someone, for example, who might now be hoping for a clear field of play in regard to Marie. Now *that* would be a powerful motive.

It all pointed to one man: the sour-faced Bavarian, Mannstein. The lazy tortoise himself.

All of this became clear in Heinrich's mind as the Kübel bounced along the dusty lanes. He was equally clear that there would come a time for scores to be settled.

But would he be around to settle them?

Not a soul was to be seen in Belville. Heinrich knew this did not mean the village was deserted or the villagers were unaware of what was happening. Far from it. The convoy would have been observed while it was still distant. A labourer in the fields, a woman trudging home from a neighbouring farm, a sharp-eyed child: someone would have seen the vehicles and passed on word of their imminent arrival, just as they always did when Heinrich came and went on his own. Eyes would be watching from every window and shadowed doorway.

He brought the Kübel to a halt outside Marie's cottage and shut down the engine. He leapt out and watched as Klemt's Mercedes, black and gleaming, glided to a halt behind the Kübel, blocking the lane. The truck stopped a little further away, needing space for the troopers to disembark.

Klemt waited until his driver had opened the door of the Mercedes for him, then he settled his cap in place and stepped out. His head turned slowly from side to side as he examined his surroundings. He was not impressed. His mouth turned down more than usual as he took in the ruined dwellings, the cracked walls, the collapsed scaffolding and failed attempts at repair, the rusting oddments of farm machinery.

'Which house?' he asked Heinrich. His lip curled.

He seemed relieved when Heinrich indicated Marie's neat and tidy dwelling.

The troopers and their leutnant, the truck driver, jumped down from the truck in a clatter of heavy boots and rifles. Klemt nodded to the leutnant, giving him the signal to proceed. Two of the troopers marched directly into the cottage; the leutnant and the others went to the yard. Klemt's driver stayed by the Mercedes and lit a cigarette.

Heinrich winced as he heard Marie's startled cry from

within the cottage.

He turned to Klemt. 'Herr Major, with respect I request –'

Klemt cut him off. 'You will request nothing. You are not in any position to make requests. You will shut up. You can manage that, I hope.'

Marie appeared in the doorway at the front of the cottage. She was supposed to look surprised and upset – that was the plan she and Heinrich had agreed – and she did: she looked utterly devastated.

Heinrich's heart went out to her. This was beyond mere play-acting; she was genuinely terrified. Not only did she know now what the danger was, explained by him on his earlier visit, but here was the reality of that threat, its physical embodiment, in this bitter-faced Gestapo officer and these armed troopers.

The search was rapid and thorough. Every corner of the cottage was examined, every cupboard emptied, their contents strewn over the floor. There were many breakages. Beds were stripped, the mattresses slashed and searched. The couch was ripped open. Heinrich could not see what was happening outside in the yard, but doubtless it and the barn were receiving similar attention.

Klemt stomped back and forth between the cottage and the yard, watching the troopers at work. He sneered as a chest of drawers was tipped over and Marie's lingerie spilled across the floor for all to see.

He made Heinrich and Marie stand in the cottage throughout, well apart, with orders to remain silent. They stared at one another. Heinrich's heart ached. He wanted to take his brave little Marie in his arms and pour all his love into her.

He also wanted to lock his hands about Klemt's

skinny neck and snap it like a dry twig.

Never once did he or Marie glance in the direction of the graveyard. Never once did Klemt or the troopers show any interest in it.

Nothing was found.

Nothing, that is, until Klemt's driver strode into the cottage. He did not come from the lane where Heinrich had last seen him, but from the yard.

'Heil Hitler! Herr Major, forgive my interruption. If you would please accompany me . . .'

Klemt showed neither surprise nor displeasure at the interruption.

'Very well.'

The driver turned on his heel and headed outside to return to the yard. Klemt followed.

Heinrich looked anxiously at Marie. She gave a small shake of her head, as mystified as he was. Since the driver had spoken in German, she had not even understood what he had said.

Klemt reappeared. He beckoned to Marie.

'Come here! Hurry up!'

For her benefit, he spoke in French, though his meaning would have been clear in any language.

Heinrich took a step forward. Klemt raised a hand to stop him.

'Not you – only her!'

Marie followed Klemt outside. She looked over her shoulder at Heinrich. He could only stare helplessly after her.

Then he waited. He heard Klemt speak, but he sounded as if he was far away. Yet he had not gone down the yard. Heinrich realised that he and Marie were in her greenhouse.

Klemt spoke again. His tone now was harsh and insistent, bullying. But when Marie replied, her tone was as determined as his. Klemt tried to interrupt her but she carried on. She spoke at some length, ignoring his further interruptions, her voice level and controlled even though it was clear that she was angry. She was arguing with him. Heinrich was torn between fear for her and admiration for her courage.

But what was going on? What was the argument about?

Eventually, they returned to the cottage. Behind them came Klemt's driver. He was carrying a case of wine. Heinrich recognised it at once – it was an exceptionally fine burgundy, a Côte de Beaune. He saw the label with the winemaker's name. He knew this wine, but only by reputation. It was a wine that would fetch a handsome price from the right customer – but he had never had that wine among his stock.

Marie was ordered back to where she had been standing previously. Her gaze never left Heinrich. There were tears in her eyes. He stared back at her. The pain in his heart was intense. His beautiful, precious Marie. There was so much he wanted to say to her.

He understood now what was happening here, though he had not yet figured out why. And perhaps never would.

Klemt was saying something to him.

'How do you explain this?' The Gestapo man had reverted to German. 'This wine is a prime example of the fine French goods that are supposed to be sent to Germany. This requirement is in accordance with the standing orders of Reichsmarschall Göring himself. So how did these bottles come to be here? Explain!'

Heinrich could almost hear the snap of the trap as it closed on him. There was no point arguing or trying to defend himself, no point denying or protesting. It was clear to him what he had to do now. As a businessman, he understood negotiation. And that was what this had become – a negotiation, a trade. The subject of that trade was Marie herself – her freedom and possibly her life.

Which meant that for him, there would be no turning back now.

'Herr Major, I confess my guilt. I'm responsible for the wine being here. I obtained it through a contact, a French civilian. I don't know his identity. Nor do I know where he can be found.'

There was triumph in Klemt's face. The admission of guilt was what he wanted. That, and only that. He was not interested in details, whether true or fabricated. And in this case, he knew they would be fabricated. They would *have* to be, since the whole situation was a nonsense of his own creation.

'Then let us be clear,' he said to Heinrich. 'Let there be no misunderstanding between us. Previously, you insisted to me that you were innocent of any wrongdoing, yes? You assured me that all allegations to the contrary were false. You were adamant on this point. Now you're taking all of that back. Yes?'

'Yes, Herr Major, that's correct. That's what I'm doing. You have the evidence against me, so I'm making a clean breast of things.'

Klemt could not resist one final taunt. He looked across the room at Marie, waiting patiently and unknowing while her fate was being determined.

'And your little French whore?'

Heinrich had that image in his mind again, of his

hands about Klemt's neck.

'Herr Major, that is not what she is – as you know. And this has nothing to do with her. She didn't even know the wine was here. The crime is mine alone. I brought those bottles here and concealed them without her knowledge.'

'She's the one who's innocent?'

'Yes, Herr Major. She's completely innocent.'

'So. Then I think we do understand one another.'

'Yes, Herr Major. I hope we do.'

After a final moment's thought, Klemt nodded. He was satisfied. The negotiation was concluded. Marie was safe.

Heinrich felt a calmness come over him, a feeling of resignation, of acceptance, of yielding to the inevitable. What would be would be. What happened to him now was not important. Marie's safety, that was what was important.

That, and his ability to withstand what would now follow. Whatever that might be, at least he would at last find out what Klemt was really after. It would be the toughest test of his life. But that was all right, he was ready for it.

The stakes could not be higher. Because despite all of Klemt's cunning, there was one victory that was still Heinrich's. It was the most important victory of all.

The Engländer had not been found.

Marie knew Heinrich had done something terrible, though she did not know what it was. Was it only to do with the wine, or did it concern the Englishman, the spy? Her few words of German were no use in helping her follow what Heinrich and the Gestapo man had been saying, but she had watched Heini's face, she saw the defeat etched on it – genuine defeat, not a pretence – and she knew he had given in and agreed to whatever it was the Gestapo man wanted.

But whatever that was, this was not what was supposed to happen. This was not what she and Heini had planned. His face told her that.

She dashed forward and flung her arms about his neck.

'No, Heini – no! Don't give in to them! It's a lie! That wine – they're lying!'

'Hush now. I know that, I understand.'

'Then why are you giving in?'

'Hush, meine Liebe.' He lowered his voice to a whisper. 'I have to do it, you see.'

He caught her hands and gently brought them down, kissed them and pressed them to his chest. She heard the Gestapo man say something, maybe he issued an order, then someone grabbed her. It was the other man, the one who had found the case of wine – except *that* was the lie, the lie was the wine and his finding of it.

The man pulled her away from Heinrich, separated them so that they were once again at a distance from each other. She shook him off and crossed her arms in fury, fists clenched. Her gaze remained locked on Heini.

The Gestapo man spoke to Heini. Heini listened and nodded, then explained to her.

'He says he'll arrest you too if you do that again. And I'm asking you not to do anything. I want you to be safe,

Marie. That's what I've agreed with him – that you're innocent, so you *will* be safe. He'll leave you alone.'

She shot a fiery look at the Gestapo man.

'You can't possibly believe that, Heini. You can't trust him. Surely you know that? He's a liar. He lies with every breath he takes.'

'I have no choice, meine Liebe. Hush now, hush.'

The Gestapo man stood there listening to their exchange. She could see he was relishing their unhappiness. She knew he had heard her accusation, every word of it. His ugly mouth twisted into what she supposed was a smile.

He said something to the troopers. Heinrich was taken out to the truck, escorted by two of the men. Someone drove his vehicle away. Marie's last sight of him was as he was pushed into the back of the truck.

'Meine Liebe!' he called.

Then the tailgate was slammed shut and bolted, and the vehicle roared away.

The Gestapo man was in no hurry to leave. He paused beside Marie to look slowly about the room on his way to the door. His gaze took in her dresses and lingerie spread over the floor and now trampled and soiled by his men's boots. His attention lingered on the most intimate garments, then he looked directly at her. It was an unhurried look, a look that made her shudder, for she knew exactly what he was thinking.

'Marie,' he said. 'Ah, Marie. Such a pretty name.' His bony finger stroked her cheek. 'It suits you very well – pretty name, pretty face. What a dear child you are. And I don't always lie, you know – you *are* such a pretty one. That's no lie, I assure you.'

Then he went outside and she heard his car drive off.

She fell to her knees against the ruined couch and

wept – long sobs that racked her body in waves. It was a long time before the tears stopped and she became silent, exhausted. A long time before she could unclench her fist and turn her attention to the keys that Heinrich had pressed into her hand during their final desperate embrace.

Archie felt as though he had become some kind of sightless, subterranean creature. He had never experienced such complete darkness. The place was thick with cobwebs that he could not see and blundered through. They clung to his face and clothes and covered his mouth. When he tried to wipe them away, he simply added more to their density.

The pain in his head was no better, but he forced himself to shuffle carefully around the confined space of the tomb until he had it mapped in his mind: wooden cases of wine and champagne along here; dust-encrusted burial caskets over there; the bronze door here. As a feat of navigation, it was a far cry from gazing down from on high at the moonlit fields of France sweeping beneath his wings, but at least it stopped him thinking endlessly about Marie. Even so, flashes of memory still intruded – the touch of her hand, the smell of her hair. He did his best to send the thoughts away, spat out more cobwebs, continued pacing the blackness.

He found a space behind some of the caskets and managed to slide his body into it – an accomplishment that filled him with revulsion but might just help him avoid capture if the Germans got into the tomb. Having confirmed that he could fit himself into the space, he exited it as swiftly as the pain of movement would allow: time enough to go there if he was forced to do so, but not until then.

But now it seemed that time had come. Keys scraped in the locks of the bronze door. He withdrew as quickly as he could towards the rear of the tomb, making for the caskets. His head roared with pain at the sudden movement.

'Archie?'

It was Marie. He could imagine no sweeter sound. The tension in his limbs evaporated. The bronze door creaked open. Fresh air flooded in. The glow of a lantern appeared. Apparently, dusk had fallen in the world outside this place. Behind the lantern, he could just make out her face. He could not have wished for any more beautiful sight.

But his caution remained. He was silent and stayed where he was.

'It's safe now,' she said. 'Where are you? I can't see you.'

She came no closer but thrust the lantern forward so that its light fell on him.

'Are you alone?' he asked her.

'Yes. They've gone, the Gestapo man and the others. There's only me, I'm completely alone. It's all right, Archie, you're safe. You can come out now.'

He believed her. He trusted her. She was not lying; she would not lie. He suspected she was actually incapable of doing so. If there was someone behind her, ready to capture him, she would have found a way to give him some hint, a warning.

But still, there was a tautness in her voice that did not feel right. And in her words there was too much emphasis on being alone. Then it dawned on him.

'Where's Heinrich?'

It took her a moment to reply. A moment in which he realised she was working at controlling her emotions.

'They arrested him. They've taken him. He managed to give me the keys, but he's gone.'

'Oh, Marie! I'm so sorry.' Such a pointless thing to say. All it did was provoke a half-stifled sob from her.

He came out from the tomb and gratefully filled his

lungs with the evening air. It seemed wrong that he should feel the relief this brought to him while she was steeped in such misery. He wanted to go to her, hold her and comfort her, but did not know how to or what he could possibly say to her. He felt useless.

His head throbbing, he followed her from the graveyard to the cottage. Here he found a scene of chaos. Her home had been torn apart.

'Heini was right.' She sighed and set the lantern down. 'They searched. And they destroyed things.'

He caught a glimpse of something that had been bundled into a drawer, saw it for an instant before she closed the drawer – hurriedly, as if she had intended to do so before fetching him. Something white. It was the garments he had seen that morning.

While he stood there staring at the wreckage about him, she was the practical one. Somehow she produced clean clothing for him from the chaos – trousers, a shirt, underwear, all items of good quality. Although they were civilian garments, he assumed they belonged to Heinrich. There was even a pair of shoes. Their fit was good enough.

This time, he stripped naked to wash at the pump while she remained indoors, allowing him privacy. He took a deep breath and stuck his head right under the pump and scrubbed the cobwebs and filth away. The pain inflicted by the cold water was excruciating, but he wanted the wound to be as clean as possible – as clean as Marie had made it before Heinrich and his Luger had undone her good work. He thought about the pain she was suffering, so he kept his groans to himself and got on with the job.

While he washed, she consigned his old clothing to the

fire, even the flying boots. He towelled himself dry, put on the fresh clothing and returned indoors to watch everything burn. It was like seeing his identity vanish.

Dusk became night as they worked together to restore some order to the little cottage. His head continued to throb, but he ignored it. Much of her food had been destroyed in the search, so they shared the bread and cheese she had stowed for him in the case of champagne. They drank wine – good wine, from Heinrich's stock – but they sipped it in restrained moderation, like nervous strangers uncertain of each other. She described all that had happened with the Gestapo officer, what he had done and how Heinrich had given in to him.

'He was protecting me, Archie – and you as well.'

Now there was silence but for the soft crackle of the fire. He watched her in the glow of the lantern. He longed to declare his feelings for her, but how could he even think of doing that while her heart so clearly ached for Heinrich?

He went out to the yard and watched the moon. Last night he had seen it rise over Tangmere. It was still almost full tonight. Perhaps someone was setting out from Tangmere at this very moment. Was anyone over there thinking about him, wondering if he was dead or captured? It was another perfect night for an operation – a perfect moon night. There was no cloud, the sky was studded with stars, and everything around him down here was as clearly visible as in daylight – the yard, the little white cottage, the ruined church and the graveyard where he had laboured and hidden among the dead.

He listened to the rhythmic whisper of the ocean. The fact was, he did not belong here. War had brought him here, it controlled him as surely as the moon controlled the tides, and war was where he belonged. It was a delusion to think that his identity had vanished. He remembered the ominous structures of the Atlantic Wall that he had seen as the Lysander made its fateful descent. They were works of evil that had to be destroyed along with the power that had created them. His duty was to get back to England and rejoin the war that would defeat that evil power. His duty was to apply his talent, to make his contribution.

He went down the yard to the barn and removed the loose concrete block at the base of the wall. His maps and the escape kit were still there where he had hidden them. But his hand encountered something else. Inexplicably, the .38 revolver and the carton of bullets were there as well.

A movement caught his eye, and he looked around to find Marie watching him. As usual, she was barefoot. He had not seen or heard her approach.

'Did you put these here?' he asked as he stood up.

She shook her head. 'Heinrich did, this morning, after he locked you up. He said you were sure to have things that were important to you, things you'd want to keep safe. He said a man on the run in enemy territory would always have such things – money, identity papers. He hadn't found anything of that sort on you when he searched you, so he decided you must have arranged a hiding place somewhere for them. It didn't take him long to find it. He knew there was a chance he might be arrested today, so he put the gun and bullets there for you. He said you'd need them. He said to tell you they're a gift from one soldier to another.' The dark eyes searched Archie's face. 'But does this mean you're leaving?'

114

'Did he give you any other messages for me?'

'No other messages. He gives me messages because he knows he can trust me.' At this, there was a note of pride in her voice, then she sighed. 'But you haven't answered my question – are you leaving, Archie?'

'I have to.'

'Now? Surely not. Not tonight. Where will you go?'

'Another village, maybe.'

'But it's impossible. This whole region is far too heavily guarded for you to travel anywhere safely. There are patrols, checkpoints. You'll be captured. You were lucky not to be captured on your way here. And which village would you go to – why do you suppose there's one that would be better than Belville? Believe me – Belville is the very best place for you.'

'If I stay here, I'm putting you in danger. They'll interrogate Heinrich –'

She was dismissive. 'Oh, you don't know Heini. He's *strong*. He'll tell them nothing.'

It was bravado. He knew it, and she knew it too. Heinrich must surely have made her understand how the Gestapo operated. He would have known what was coming his way, and so must she.

But she persisted.

'Wait here a few days, Archie. Take time to think things over. Here is where you're safe. At least stay for tonight. See what tomorrow brings.'

And now she looked away from him.

'Please, Archie. I don't want to be alone tonight.'

So that was the truth of it. How had he not seen?

'Perhaps you're right after all,' he said. 'Perhaps I should rest, give my body a chance to recover.'

'Yes, Archie. You should do that.'

Both of the cottage's mattresses had been ripped open in the search. He repacked their rag filling as best he could and turned them so that the ripped side was underneath. He put one in place in her bedroom and the other in the room that had been Heinrich's storeroom. She found sheets and made the beds ready. But as they were retiring to their separate rooms, she hesitated.

'Can we keep our bedroom doors open? Then if I wake in the night, I'll be able to see I'm not alone.'

'Yes, we can do that.'

She smiled, stepped towards him and kissed him on the cheek, a kiss as light and tentative as the caress of a feather. Then she was gone, to her bedroom. He heard the quiet sounds of her undressing and climbing into bed. The light of the lantern dimmed and faded to nothing as she extinguished it, leaving the rooms to the moonlight. Within minutes, she was fast asleep. For a time, he remained standing there, listening to her steady breathing and the soft noises she made in her sleep. Then he went to his own bed.

Her praise for Heinrich had stung him, along with her pride and confidence in the German. But what did Archie expect? It was clear that Heinrich was her whole world. And Archie knew he could hardly begrudge the man. On the contrary, even with that crack on the head, he was in the German's debt.

Heinrich had in fact left him a further message, a very private one that Marie did not know about. He had done it by the simple act of putting the revolver and bullets in Archie's hiding place rather than leaving them with Marie. He wanted Archie to know he had second-guessed him all the way – had second-guessed Marie as well by anticipating that she would persuade Archie to stay. One soldier to another, he had said – it was not the first time he had made the remark. He was telling Archie that they found themselves on opposing sides in this war but that did not mean they had to be enemies. Marie had rescued Archie, taken him into her care; now Heinrich was entrusting Marie to Archie's care. That was the message. From one soldier to another.

The cottage was quiet, the night peaceful, the rise and fall of the surf as gentle as a lullaby. Archie heard Marie sigh softly in her sleep. He wanted morning never to come.

Cold steel woke him. Cold steel against his forehead. The muzzle of a gun.

He had been drifting in and out of sleep, never sure whether he was awake or dreaming. Perhaps he was asleep now. Perhaps this was only a dream.

The gun pressed harder. It scraped against his wound. Pain ripped through him. This was no dream. His vision cleared, all sleep gone. Someone was standing over him, a silhouette against the moonlight.

'Englishman!'

The word hit him like a slap. Apart from Marie and Heinrich, the only people who knew he was English were those who were hunting him: his German pursuers.

'Don't move, Englishman. Not a muscle, not until I say.'

He tasted last night's wine in his mouth, but it was sour now, vinegar. He cursed his stupidity. In agreeing to stay, he had succumbed to his own desire to be with Marie and had allowed himself to remain in her home where anyone could find him. He had been weak. He should have slipped away while she slept and hidden himself somewhere well away from her – in that dreadful tomb, perhaps.

Now he would pay for his folly. Worse, far worse, so would Marie. So much for having her in his care; so much for fulfilling Heinrich's trust in him.

The voice spoke again. But this time not to him. It called out in the direction of Marie's bedroom.

'Marie! Come on, Marie – time to wake up!'

The voice was female. There was no trace of a German accent. And its owner was evidently on first-name terms with Marie.

From the other room, he heard the sounds of Marie stirring.

'Simone? Is that you? What are you doing here? It's the middle of the night!'

'Get up, Marie.'

She appeared in the doorway. She was dishevelled but had dressed and was drawing a shawl about her shoulders.

'You're crazy, Simone! What are you doing with that gun? Put it away!'

Simone stepped back from Archie's bed. The gun was no longer pressing against his head, but it remained trained on him.

'Your turn now, Englishman – if that's what you really are. Up you get.'

He glanced over at the place on the floor where he had left his revolver last night. The weapon was gone. More evidence of his carelessness.

'Don't worry about your gun. I'm looking after it. You don't need it.'

'You don't need yours, either,' Marie told her. She was now awake enough to be angry. 'This is my home and you have no right to come creeping into it like a thief in the night – like a murderer, waving that gun about.'

Simone ignored her. She prodded Archie at gunpoint from the bedroom. A match flared as Marie lit the lantern, supplementing the moonlight. Now Archie could see Simone clearly, not just in silhouette. She was tall and slim. A square face with calm, watchful eyes. She was wearing trousers and a man's suit jacket that hung loosely on her frame. He judged her to be in her thirties. Her hair, though dark, was prematurely streaked with grey. But rather than ageing her, it gave her an air of distinction, even authority.

She saw the wound on Archie's head.

'A nasty injury, that. How did you get it?'

Archie glared at her. 'You didn't improve it. A German bullet did it. Then pistol-whipped by a German Luger.'

'Heinrich's weapon, he did it,' Marie told her. 'Not that it's any of your business.'

Simone clucked her tongue. 'Heinrich must have had a reason. He's a good man. Perhaps you and he fell out, Englishman. Perhaps you provoked him.'

'I didn't provoke him. We didn't fall out. It wasn't like that.'

'Then tell me how it was.'

'Why should I tell you anything? Who are you?'

'I'm a friend of Marie's –'

Marie snorted. 'You're not behaving like one.'

'Possibly your friend too, Englishman. But only possibly. We'll see.'

'My friend too? What kind of friend holds me at gunpoint?'

'The kind whose friendship depends on what they learn about you.'

'You seem to know a good deal already.'

'I do. But are they true, the things I know? Tell me what happened with Heinrich.'

Archie looked to Marie for guidance. She sighed and nodded for him to answer.

'I can only tell you that whatever Heinrich was up to, he was in a great hurry. I think he just wanted me out of the way quickly and with no trouble. I guess knocking me senseless was as good a way as any to achieve that.'

Marie nodded in confirmation. 'Heini was helping me to hide him. I talked him into doing that. He knew my cottage might be searched, and there were things he needed to do before that happened. Time was already short for him – with someone to hide, it was even shorter. That's why he was in a hurry.'

'You're telling me Heinrich helped to hide this man, this Englishman? Why would he do that? Heinrich is German. Good man though he is, a German is a German. Why did he take that risk?'

'I told you – I talked him into it. He did it for my sake. I was sheltering an enemy of the Reich and I would have been shot for that. Heini was protecting me.'

'And himself as well, perhaps?'

'I suppose so. He said he would be considered as guilty as me – so, yes, you could say he was protecting himself as well.'

Simone seemed persuaded by Marie's explanation, but she continued to take no chances. She ordered Archie and Marie to sit at the table while she remained on her feet and in control of them and the room. The place was still in some disarray. She lowered her gun but continued to ignore Marie's requests to put it away, prowling the room with it in her hand.

'Why did you come here, Englishman? Why Belville?'

'I wanted to find a priest to give me protection. I didn't want to risk being betrayed if I approached anyone else for help. We're told that's the safest thing to do – find a priest.'

Simone grunted sceptically. 'Safest for you, perhaps, though not necessarily for Belville. But it's too late now to do anything about that. What's done is done. Everyone in Belville knows you're here. We knew from the moment you arrived. You were trying so hard to be invisible, but we saw you, many of us did. And those who didn't see you for themselves were told of your arrival by those who did. So everyone knows – which for you is a good thing. It means that no one will be taken by surprise and there'll be no questions asked, nothing blurted out at the wrong time for the wrong people to hear. That's how things are here, you see. That's our way, in Belville – we're careful. You should consider yourself fortunate.'

'I do, of course.'

'This is simply how Belville is. We have our secrets but not from each other. Belville has suffered – look around you at the homes that have been destroyed; look at our church and the school. Death has walked among us, so we like to know what's going on in our village and who's involved. Belville looks after its own. We keep our eyes and ears open and our mouths shut.'

'I see.'

'But do you? Because there are things about you, Englishman, that have to be explained. I've told you about Belville, but we need to know for certain who you are. You might be a Boche agent, a spy. You might be a trap. Belville is good at keeping secrets, and we'll keep your secret, never fear – if you are who you say you are. We have no priest, but you'll be safe under our protection. But in coming here, you endanger us. So don't take our protection for granted.'

Archie tried to make sense of what he was hearing and seeing. It was a struggle.

First there was Marie, whose relationship with Heinrich was hardly that of enemies at war, of occupier and occupied. And now here was this Simone, whose authority Marie seemed to accept, who spoke of Heinrich as a good man and who seemed to be as well disposed to him as Marie was. But in the same breath, Simone was also talking about German spies and traps. Traps to catch

122

whom? And set by whom? Who was on whose side here in Belville? How could Heinrich, a German, be regarded as a good man while Archie could come under suspicion as a possible German spy? Who was this Simone, and why should she care if Archie was working for the Germans? What was that to her? How would it be different from Marie's relationship with Heinrich?

Most disconcerting of all, how did Simone know he was English? What else did she know, and why had she come here tonight to investigate him?

It seemed that Simone had questions of her own. She turned her attention to Marie.

'That Gestapo snake who came here – that's another thing that needs to be explained. If Herr Gestapo had been looking for this Englishman of yours, he would have razed Belville to the ground to find him. But all he did was arrest Heinrich. So was it only Heinrich's little business sideline that interested him? Was that the only reason why Herr Gestapo was here?'

Marie considered this question.

'I think so. He found no evidence, so he planted some and arrested Heinrich on a lie. That way, he got what he wanted. I think that was his plan all along. That's what brought him here.'

'Such a fuss over a little black market! You'd think Herr Gestapo would have better ways of amusing himself, more important crimes to investigate. He missed something far more valuable than a few cases of cognac – he missed this English airman, the very man he himself had been searching for only a few hours earlier.'

Archie could not conceal his surprise. Yet again this woman seemed to know so much – more than he himself knew.

Simone made no secret of enjoying his reaction. The watchful eyes creased in amusement.

'Don't look so shocked, Englishman. Yes, we know you're an airman – apparently. We know what happened to you – assuming you are who you claim to be. You see how we have these doubts? We must be careful. But what we do know for a fact is that the Boche spent last night looking for you – well, to be exact, they were looking for the person you claim to be – and we know that Herr Gestapo himself joined the search. We also know that Heinrich was one of the searchers. It was what he was doing after leaving here in the middle of the night.'

Marie nodded. 'He told me that.'

'And he hurried back here because, as you said, Marie, he knew somehow that this cottage was to be searched. My guess is, he came here to get rid of potential evidence – not evidence about you, Englishman, but evidence of his little black market.'

Again Marie agreed. 'He called it making precautionary arrangements.'

'And he made them well – which is why Herr Gestapo found nothing.'

Archie thought about his labours for Heinrich. 'I'm the one who did the work.'

'Are you complaining? Heinrich saved your English skin.'

'And I certainly have no complaints. But how do you know who I am? How do you know about the search?'

'Don't concern yourself with that. For you, all that counts is getting back to England. That's what you want, isn't it? At least, I suppose that's what you would have me believe.'

Back to England. They were the last words Archie

expected to hear. They had their effect not only on him but on Marie as well. He heard her sudden intake of breath. But when he looked at her, her face revealed nothing.

Simone had also heard that sharp breath and had caught Archie's glance. He and Simone looked at one another. Neither made any comment. For that brief moment, they were co-conspirators.

Archie broke the silence. 'Are you saying you know how I can get back to England?'

'I'm saying more than that, Englishman. I'm saying there is no other way.'

'No other way than with your help?'

'Correct. You'll have to trust me. And you must be patient. These things can take time.'

'How much time?'

'Impossible to say.'

'Then I'll make my own way.'

'Bad idea.'

'The longer I stay here, the more dangerous it is for Marie.'

Marie was shaking her head. 'That's not true. I'll be safe. Tell him, Simone.'

Simone agreed. 'Marie is right. Belville –'

Archie sighed. 'Yes, I know. Belville looks after its own. You said.'

'Because it's true, Englishman. And there's another consideration.'

'What?'

'If you are who you say you are, if you try to make your way by yourself, you'll be captured. I guarantee that. And then you'll tell the Boche everything – including this conversation and my part in it. I guarantee that too, and I won't allow it. My comrades won't allow it.'

'Meaning?'

Now Simone stopped prowling. Her gun was trained on him again.

'Meaning I'll shoot you if I have to. Just like I'll shoot you if you turn out to be a Boche spy.'

Unlike Heinrich, Simone wanted details of Archie's identity. She passed a pencil and a small notebook to Marie so that she could record everything. The pistol stayed in Simone's hand, a reminder to Archie that he was still under scrutiny and unproven. As well as his name, date of birth, rank and service number, Simone wanted to know his squadron number and where he was based, the squadron letters of his aircraft and the individual aircraft letter. He assumed she had some way of verifying through checks of some kind what he was telling her. Some parts of the information she demanded would have been easy enough for the Germans to obtain, but others, such as his aircraft letter, were not.

He answered all her questions until she asked about the operation that had brought him to France.

'That stays secret,' was his response.

She sighed. 'Then tell me about the dead man.'

'What dead man?'

'Please don't play games, Archie. My information is that the Boche found a dead man at the crash site. If he wasn't the pilot, if that's what you are, then who or what was the dead man?'

Archie shook his head.

'I have to know,' she insisted.

'I don't have to tell you.'

'Did your operation concern this region, this part of Normandy?'

'It didn't. That much I can tell you. The operation was a long way from here. I had completed it successfully, but there was an ambush and my aircraft was damaged. I was returning to England when I crashed. That's the only reason I ended up in this part of Normandy – and that's all I'll tell you.'

She was unhappy but could see she would not budge him. However, that did not mean she was finished with him.

'Do you have an escape kit? Give it to me.'

This was another demand too far.

'I need it.'

'No, you don't. You're not going anywhere – not until I make the necessary arrangements. *If* I do. And then you still won't need the escape kit – we'll provide everything you need. If you're found with the kit or any recognisable part of it, your fate will be sealed – you might as well hang a sign around your neck announcing you're an English agent, a spy. I imagine you have ID photographs? Let me see them.'

He did so. She took them from him, giving them only the most cursory of glances.

'These are useless,' she declared. 'Worse than useless because they're dangerous. They make you look exactly like what you are – a healthy young Englishman who's never missed a square meal, never lived in a permanent state of fear from one day to the next. Look at these photographs – do *you* think you look like you've spent four years trying to survive Nazi occupation? The Boche would take one look at these and that would be the end of you.'

She dropped the photographs onto the glowing embers of the fire.

Loïc Boiteux's identity card caught her eye. She studied it for a few moments, then smiled at Archie. A little smile of success. He shrugged. Let her have her dead man. She slipped the card into her pocket. Perhaps it too would now be part of her checks, whether or not it was genuine.

She also pocketed the twenty thousand francs plus Loïc's oddments of cash – 'We always need funds' – then tipped the rest of the escape kit into the fire except for the penknife, which she kept.

'You speak of your comrades,' Archie said. 'Who are they?'

'You have your secrets. I have mine.'

'Are you the Resistance?'

'You can call us that if you like.'

'Yet you seem to think highly of Heinrich.'

Archie kept an eye on Marie as he spoke. In effect, he was asking about her and Heinrich. But her face remained as unreadable as before.

He continued with Simone. 'A German is a German, you said. So doesn't that make Heinrich your enemy?'

Simone shook her head. 'How much you fail to understand. Hitler is our enemy. The Gestapo are our enemy. Nazis are our enemy. The ignorant Boche who blindly follow Hitler and his Nazis are our enemy. Tragically, some of our own French citizens – and many of our political leaders – are our enemy. But not Heinrich. He's not our enemy. Tell me this – has he been your enemy? No, of course not. He lives his life and lets us live ours. He's good to Marie, and that means a lot here in Belville. Like all of us, he didn't choose to be caught up in this war. Like all of us, he does what he

128

can to make life tolerable.'

Marie sat quietly listening. Simone produced a pack of cigarettes and lit one. It was a Reemtsma.

'Do you get those from Heinrich?'

She drew deeply on the cigarette. 'As a matter of fact, I do. And the occasional bottle of cognac if you want to know. Also my Chanel perfume to cheer myself up, when I can afford it. He sells mostly to Germans, of course, but I'm not his only French customer. Not just in Belville. Perhaps you think that makes us collaborators. Resistance or collabos, you ask – which are we? Let me think about that, how should I answer? Perhaps we're both.' Again, she enjoyed his puzzlement. 'But you could just as easily say that Heinrich collaborates with us. So he's a collabo too. Try looking at it that way.'

She was quiet for a moment, her thoughts turning inward. Her mood seemed to darken.

'You have to realise, Archie, this isn't England. Your country isn't under occupation, so you don't know what that's like. Life here is complicated. There are many strands, and they intertwine in many ways. One of these days, when the Boche are defeated and we kick them out of France, that will be the time for us to separate the strands into the good and the bad. That will be the time to make judgements – this man good, this woman bad, this person our friend, this one our foe, this one a traitor, a collabo. But not now. Not yet. For now, the strands are the only things holding everything together. They're all we have.'

He saw the sadness that settled itself on her as she spoke, and he knew that Marie too saw her change of mood. This was no longer Simone the bold adventurer, the commanding force. He had no doubt she knew how to use that pistol – had no doubt she *had* used it in her time and would do so again when she had to – but at this moment she was no longer the confident fighter. This Simone was a woman who had lost what gave her life meaning and defined her. She had lost her country.

Dawn was silvering the sky. Marie opened the door to the yard, bringing fresh air and the sound of birdsong into the cottage. She stoked the fire and went outside to wash herself and fetch water.

At long last, Simone put her pistol away. But she showed no inclination to return Archie's revolver to him.

'Not until I've checked you out.'

So now at least he knew his guess was correct – she had some way of verifying the information he had given her.

'And the next step?'

'You wait to hear from me. You stay here with Marie. I don't think you'll find that too disagreeable.' She gave him a measuring look. 'But I advise you to tread carefully. For Marie's sake.'

'What do you mean?'

'Marie is little more than a child. She's vulnerable, fragile. Heinrich has been her rock, but he's gone now and he won't be coming back. In his absence, she might turn to you for comfort, support. If she does, I hope you wouldn't take advantage of that. I hope you wouldn't misinterpret –'

He felt a sudden flare of anger. 'I don't think I need your advice.'

'Don't you? You've known Marie for how long – a few hours? Yet already you've spent the night here with her, just the two of you. You have to admit, you didn't lose any time.'

Enough was enough, however important this woman might be in getting him back to England.

'That's none of your business, Simone. Don't assume things of which you have no knowledge – and no right to have any such knowledge.'

'I'm simply telling you to be careful. She's had too much hurt in her life as it is. And now she's lost Heinrich. Don't cause her more hurt. You're here today, gone tomorrow.'

'And all I want from you is exactly that – to help me be gone as soon as possible. Do what's necessary to get me to England and keep your advice about Marie to yourself. Despite what you may think, she's an adult. She knows her own mind, she'll make her own decisions – if ever any decisions have to be made.'

'Then at least let me explain. You need to understand what Marie has been through.'

'I'm listening.'

She lit another cigarette. 'There was a bombing raid on Caen. Just over a year ago. English aircraft, piloted by your fellow countrymen. One of them made a mistake. A navigational error, perhaps; we don't know. All we know is the consequence. The aircraft dropped some of its bombs on Belville. That's how our homes and church and school were destroyed. Many of our villagers died that night, including children. Heinrich brought a unit of his men here and organised a rescue operation to dig people from the rubble. As you can imagine, some of his men were far from happy about that – the last thing they wanted to do was rescue French citizens when their own comrades had been bombed. We heard afterwards that they reported Heinrich to his superiors, but somehow he got away with it. He has that knack, of getting away with things. It's certain that many more people would have died beneath the rubble if it hadn't been for him.'

'Why did he help – because of Marie?'

Simone shook her head. 'He didn't know her then, they hadn't met. Marie's mother and father were among those who lost their lives that night. They were in the church with the priest and some of the older village children, preparing it for Easter. All of them were killed – the priest, Marie's mother and father, the children, all of them Marie's friends who had grown up with her. It was Heinrich himself who recovered the bodies of Marie's parents, and it was he who broke the news to her. Those were the circumstances under which they came to know one another.'

'Was that when he began using the graveyard and her cottage for storage?'

She nodded. 'Soon afterwards. Until then, all he had was an abandoned railcar at one of the Atlantic Wall construction sites. Belville is better.'

'Belville looks after its own.'

A wry smile. 'At last you're learning. And now you know everything.'

It was clear that she had no more to say. She finished her cigarette, then dropped the butt into the fire and went out to the yard to take her leave of Marie. They spoke together quietly for a minute or two, then kissed cheeks. Simone departed.

Marie came back indoors. Her eyes were bright as she smiled at Archie. His heart lifted at the sight of her. She was beautiful, so beautiful. But it was more than physical beauty alone. The real beauty was in her innocent heart and soul.

'Simone says you're going to stay here, Archie. In Belville, with me. She says you don't need to go anywhere else. I'm glad about that. Are you?'

'Yes, I am, Marie. I'm glad. Very glad.'

And it was the truth – just as in his heart he knew there was truth in what Simone had said about Marie's vulnerability: Truth also in Simone's warnings to him. Her account of what Heinrich had done explained many things about the relationship between the German and Belville – and his relationship with Marie especially. But there were matters on which Archie was still none the wiser. Why had Heinrich helped Belville that night? He must have known his men would object, yet he went ahead with the rescue.

And now the German had protected him. Why?

'You know everything,' Simone had said.

Not quite. Not by a long way.

So many strands, intertwined.

Klemt's men had brought Heinrich to the Gestapo man's headquarters, the barracks in Caen, and dumped him in this cell. It was just large enough for him to manage four paces in each direction. The walls, floor and ceiling were bare concrete. One small window, barred and unglazed, too high for him to reach, allowed him to see only a rectangle of sky and the topmost boughs of a ragged pine tree. He could hear the sounds of day-to-day military activity in the barracks compound outside, reminding him that life was carrying on without him. These were the limits of his world.

A light bulb protected by a metal cage burned constantly through the hours of darkness, with no switch inside the room to turn it off. The bed was a crude wooden frame bolted to the floor and supporting a thin mattress stuffed with horsehair. It was marked with brown stains, like a map of unknown lands. He had a suspicion that the stains were dried blood. There were similar stains on the blanket he had been issued and on the floor. Names and dates were scratched on the walls where previous occupants had made their bids for immortality. Some had preferred obscenities.

A steel bucket with a lid stood in one corner as a latrine. It stank to high heaven. There was no chair, no table. There were no washing facilities. He had no change of clothing, and his belt had been confiscated, presumably in case he should take a notion to hang himself. The guards had also taken his cigarettes.

Aside from that patch of sky and the branches of the weary pine tree, all he saw of the outside world was when he carried the latrine bucket across the compound to empty it into the even more stomach-turning septic tank that accommodated all the effluent from the barracks. He did this under armed guard. Troopers in the compound stared at him as he passed with his noxious burden. The stench that rose from the tank in the hot summer air made him gag. His eyes watered. The two guards gagged and wiped their eyes. Unsurprisingly, they detested these visits to the septic tank as much as he did, the consequence being that they detested him all the more.

Each morning and evening, the door of his cell would open and a guard would set a tray of food on the floor – thin soup, bread, some cheese or ham, and a tin cup of water. The arrival of these meals was the only thing that punctuated the monotony of his days.

The guards never spoke to him. In fact, no one ever spoke to him, for he had not seen or heard from Klemt since the day of his arrest.

Everything that was being done to him was part of the softening-up process. He knew this perfectly well. No interrogation: not yet. No violence: not yet. This was the first stage. The isolation, the humiliation, the denial of any means of basic personal hygiene, even the tantalising sounds of the world outside: these were all intended to break his spirit. No human contact, no conversation, no mental distractions or stimulation. His progressively weakening mind would contemplate over and over the error of his ways, until he drove himself witless obsessing about what was going to happen to him and when the punishment and interrogation might begin in earnest, fearing the worst and imagining what terrors were in store.

Klemt's absence from the scene was also a deliberate part of the process, of course – to keep Heinrich wondering and worrying, yes, but also so that when the Gestapo major did eventually appear, he would seem like a saviour, a friend, rather than his tormentor, and Heinrich would be ready to pour his guilt-laden heart out to him.

Such was the theory. Klemt's theory. A Gestapo theory. But it was a stupid theory that was not working and was never going to work.

'Not with me,' Heinrich assured himself. 'It won't work with Heinrich Hauser.' He would not be consumed by self-loathing merely because he needed a bath. He would not be obsessed by any of the imagined terrors Klemt might wish; he would not lose his mind or throw himself at the Gestapo man's feet and beg for mercy.

The only thing that troubled him was Marie. His sweet Marie. God in heaven, how he missed her. Was she safe? Had the Engländer understood his message?

The Engländer and Marie. Heinrich stared at these four concrete walls, but what he kept seeing was the Engländer and Marie, the pair of them together. Always together.

There was a price to be paid for everything.

Heavy footsteps approached. The door of the cell was unlocked, bolts were slid back, and the door crashed open. A tray was slid across the floor. Breakfast had arrived. The door closed and was locked and bolted. He stayed sitting on the bed. He preferred to wait a while before tackling the food, in order to break the monotony of the long day ahead.

But this morning that was a mistake. A few moments later, the door crashed open again and both guards entered. One of them kicked the tray away.

'On your feet! Now!'

They marched him out of the cell and along the

corridor that led to the compound. But they turned right instead of left and marched him up two flights of stairs. They made up for their days of silence by shouting at him all the way. When he stumbled, they kicked him in his side, his back, his legs, and hauled him to his feet and flung him forward to get him under way again, shouting at him all the while.

They took him along another corridor on this upper floor. Several doors led off it. They propelled him so hard through an open doorway that he stumbled again. Once more, he felt the force of their boots. He wondered what internal organs were being damaged. When he touched his face, his hand was bloody.

When they got him back on his feet, he saw that Klemt was waiting for him. The Gestapo major stood beside a desk at the side of the room, motionless and silent, his arms folded, a bone-thin, still presence in contrast with the noisy violence of Heinrich's arrival.

But Klemt was not alone. A very large soldier, a corporal, a giant of a man, was with him. This man was rolling up his sleeves. He grinned cheerfully at Heinrich. A perfectly affable grin, as if they were the best of friends. He cracked his knuckles and flexed his fists. Surely it was Heinrich's imagination that made those fists seem so huge?

The guards clicked their heels.

'Heil Hitler!'

Klemt reciprocated and the guards withdrew.

It was not easy for Heinrich to remain standing unassisted, but he forced himself to do so. The kicks had twisted his body into strange angles that he could not correct. He took in as much of the room as he could see without turning his body, which would have been too ambitious a manoeuvre to attempt.

In the centre of the room was an upright wooden chair. It was not an ordinary chair. It was not a chair that had been designed to please the eye or provide comfort for the user. There was no padding on the seat or arms or back. Its back was as high as the head of the sitter. It was exceptionally sturdy, constructed of thick unfinished timber. It was fitted with a number of leather straps at key points – where the sitter's legs, arms, chest and neck would be.

At the far end of the room, there was a large tank of water. A drowning tank. There were handcuffs and shackles fixed to the walls. There were various wooden rods and iron bars on display. There were bludgeons and truncheons of dense, hard rubber.

'You will sit,' ordered Klemt.

Heinrich did not see the corporal move. All he knew was that a cannonball seemed to have been discharged directly into his solar plexus. It was one of the corporal's mighty fists.

The pain was one thing, but worse than that was Heinrich's conviction that he would never breathe again. He gasped and tried to suck air into his lungs, but he could not make his chest expand, and no air reached them.

The corporal caught him as his legs folded and set him on the wooden chair as gently as a mother helping her infant. Heinrich continued choking and gulping for air like a stranded fish. The corporal patted his shoulder reassuringly.

'You'll be fine. It just takes a little while for things to settle. You'll see.'

He grinned down at Heinrich even more broadly than

before. Then he set about fastening the leather straps: arms, chest, legs, and finally, neck. When he was done, he tugged at each strap to check that it was snug. The grin announced his satisfaction, the satisfaction of a craftsman with a job well done.

'Comfortable?' said Klemt to Heinrich.

Fear crawled over Heinrich. He tried to fix his thoughts on Marie; he could not transport his body from here, but perhaps his mind could escape if he kept thinking hard enough about Marie.

'So,' said Klemt. He sat himself down at the desk. In contrast with his previous interview with Heinrich, this time the Gestapo man had equipped himself with several pages of notes and a writing pad. He arranged these items on the desk and uncapped a fountain pen. He tested the nib on the pad of paper, then inscribed the date neatly at the top of the page.

'We begin.'

The second stage, the interrogation proper, was under way.

Heinrich prepared himself for what was about to happen, thinking as hard as he could about Marie.

The corporal's fist swung again.

But Heinrich was past caring. His plan was working, though not quite as he had intended. For there with his sweet Marie was the Engländer.

Day by day, Marie's life gradually resumed its normal course. Her usual domestic duties were there for her as before, comforting in their solid familiarity. She busied herself with them, her instinct still to be a good Hausfrau.

She missed Heinrich. Although they had been lovers in act and deed – he was her first and only lover – she had never been *in* love with him. She would be forever grateful for all he had done for her, but gratitude was not being in love. She had known he was in love with her – a selfless love that never expected anything in return. So when she gave herself to him, it was with all the tenderness she was capable of. She wanted happiness for him.

But now he was gone, and it was as though part of her heart had been torn from her. He would never come back.

In her grief, emotions that she did not always understand flowed through her. 'Dance with me,' she told Archie one evening as they were finishing dinner. She took the glass of wine from his hand and set it down on the table.

He frowned. 'What are you up to?'

She enjoyed it when he did not know what to make of her. He was so serious, always so serious. She drew him to his feet and hummed a melody as she coaxed him into a gentle waltz. She steered him along the route that Heinrich and she used to follow around the couch and the table, all the way out to the yard. The grass was cool beneath her bare feet; lavender perfumed the air.

By the time their little dance ended – not in fits of laughter as with Heini, not in a tangle of arms and legs on her bed, but in mock-solemn bows – she realised that somehow she had said farewell to Heinrich. She began to sob. Archie put his arms about her. He did not ask why she wept. Surely he knew. When no more tears were left, she sat close beside him on the couch, rested her head on his shoulder and allowed herself to fall asleep like a child.

He was with her now through every day and night in a way that had never been possible for Heinrich. She welcomed this but knew it could not last. She dreaded Simone's return. She did not want to hear that arrangements had been made to get Archie back to England.

She tried to understand him. He was so different from Heinrich. Heini had been driven by an impatient energy that made him need to be always busy, always planning his next business deal, while Archie was happy to be still and quiet, to lose himself in the books he found on the shelf by the fireplace – books that had belonged to Maman, volumes by Victor Hugo.

'I never liked those books,' she said. 'Quasimodo gave me nightmares.'

She marvelled at Archie's patience as he worked his way through one or other of the books in what for him was a foreign language. Sometimes he asked her to explain a word or phrase, and she was pleased and flattered to become the teacher for a while.

A special kind of intimacy developed between them. He seemed to understand the things that were important to her. He helped her in her kitchen garden, digging and potting and planting. He went with her when she visited the graveyard to place fresh flowers on Maman and Papa's grave but left her by herself while she prayed. He was happy for her to greet her neighbours and spend time with them but never accompanied her and always stayed out of the way if they came calling. It was safer like that, he said.

'But these people can be trusted, Archie. Surely you know that by now.'

'But why would I want to be with anyone but you?'

She caught her breath. It was as close as he had ever come to admitting feelings for her.

He answered her questions when she asked about his life in England and he listened attentively when she spoke of her childhood and her parents. Sometimes, in these days and evenings they were now spending together, hours might pass without either of them speaking more than a dozen words. Yet she felt that their silence bound them as closely to each other as any physical act of love. It was as if he was showing her how they could be quiet together, how to be still in the way that came naturally to him and the reward that such stillness of spirit brought. In that, he was the teacher.

But as for physical acts of love, there were none. Neither act nor deed. Nor any explanation of that one admission he had made. This was the Archie she could not fathom. She remembered how he had been that first day, how his gaze followed her as she moved about her kitchen – and it still did that, he still watched her, glancing up from his book to look at her but quickly looking away if she met his gaze. But was she wrong in how she was interpreting that gaze? Was she assuming too much?

Each night as they went to their separate bedrooms, they kissed cheeks – gently, fleetingly, but his touch was enough for her to sense that he wanted her there, near him in the night while they still had time to be together, just as much as she wanted him to be there for her. She sensed also that he wanted to go further than that chaste kiss on her cheek, but he made no move to do so.

He was a mystery to her.

But she knew she was falling in love.

Archie felt time slipping away from him. The moon waned to a thin crescent and finally was gone completely. The night sky belonged to the stars.

Reports came to Belville of attacks on German patrols. Were they Simone's handiwork? But when Archie asked Marie, she merely shook her head.

'How would I know, Archie?'

As the days passed, he had the sensation of drifting in an unreal world: around him were the smells and sounds of early summer, of life being renewed; he was not being hunted down like an animal; there was food on the table; best of all, here was Marie, right here with him. There was happiness for him here, all the happiness a man could possibly wish for, and as easily grasped as berries in a hedgerow.

He knew it was all an illusion. He was still a wanted man, an enemy in German-occupied territory, at constant risk of arrest, torture and execution. The same risk applied to Marie. All it would take to make that danger a reality was a single slip by one of the villagers of Belville. In effect, his life – and therefore Marie's as well – was in the hands of every small child playing in the dusty lanes of Belville. Or there was the possibility of German reprisals for Resistance actions, whether or not they were Simone's work. The sooner he could leave, the better – and the sooner Marie would be safe.

Besides, he knew he had no right to seize any happiness, real or imagined. His only entitlement was war. He had to get back to England, had to return to the fray, resume the fight, play his part – all those noble images that were forever chasing through his head.

But Marie was dismissive of his noble thoughts. Pompous, she called them when he tried to explain.

'Why should you go back?' she challenged. 'It's not just going back to England, it's going back to war.'

'That's why I have to do it. Surely you can see that.'

'I don't see it, I don't see it at all. I don't see why anyone in their right mind would go back to war when they'd only just managed to escape it. You're not a coward; you didn't run away. You were shot down but you survived. You've been lucky – so why throw your luck away, why waste it?'

Why indeed. It would mean parting from her, which was the last thing in the world he wanted to do. But that made him no different from the countless other men and women who were forced to part from their loved ones in order to go to war. Why should he have a choice that was denied to them?

They sat outside watching the stars in the moonless sky, the cottage behind them in darkness. A gentle breeze rose and fell, bringing the smell of the ocean, sharp and clean. He heard the hiss of the surf. He also heard the catch in Marie's voice. He realised that tears were not far away. She *was* vulnerable, so very vulnerable, just as Simone had warned.

'I have to go back, Marie. It's my duty.'

'Heini used to say he had his duty. Look what it got him.'

She let the subject drop – for the time being. He knew she would return to it. But why did she argue so forcefully against his return to England; why was she so opposed to that? Could it possibly mean she had the kind of feelings for him that he had never dared to hope for – and still did not dare to consider? What else could account for her quick anger whenever he spoke of leaving? What else might explain her small sighs as they sat together in the quiet of their evenings? When they kissed cheeks to bid each other goodnight, did a shiver run through her, or was that only his imagination?

So many questions.

No answers.

But the cold fact was that nothing had changed since that night when he watched her face in the glow of the lantern and understood that no good could come from any declaration of love by him. Any day now, he would be out of her life forever – or so part of him hoped or at least accepted – so where was the point in leading her on or revealing his feelings to her? That would simply be adding to her pain when he left her. He had no right to do that to her.

Yet not letting her know the truth was lying to her by omission, allowing her to believe she was not important to him. Nothing could be further from that truth, but it was a truth he had to face alone.

It was like being in that awful tomb all over again. Whichever way he turned, wherever he looked, there seemed to be no right answer, no guiding ray of light, no way out. Only impenetrable darkness.

Was love meant to be like this?

And so, with no solution to his dilemma, he shared Marie's days and nights and the small ordinary moments of her daily life. He lived under her roof with her, the two of them as close to one another in terms of physical proximity as two people could possibly be. He did these things just as a lover would.

But never confessed his love. And never allowed himself to become the lover he longed to be.

Part Three
Angel

The month of May was all but gone, and still there was no word from Simone. Archie's restlessness intensified.

'What's become of her?' he asked Marie. 'Where is she?'

Marie shrugged. He knew by now that this was a line of questioning in which she had no interest.

'I don't know, Archie. Her absence isn't unusual. She's often away from Belville.'

'Where does she go? To do what – kill Germans?'

'I don't know that either. I don't think anyone knows. People don't ask. People don't talk about it.'

'But she *is* Resistance, right? Is she the only one in Belville, or are there others?'

He knew by now what the answer would be.

'We don't know. We don't ask. We let things be.'

Yet Simone had claimed that the people of Belville had no secrets from each other. He accepted that Marie was telling the truth as she understood it, but he was sure there were those in Belville who did know where Simone was and exactly what she was doing. Some might even be the comrades she had referred to.

As the month came to an end, his suspicions were at last confirmed.

He had decided he should get himself into reasonable physical shape for whatever would lie ahead when Simone finally sent him on his way. It might be a long overland trek. So as the injury to his head healed and he felt stronger, he began a programme of physical exercises out in the yard – simple activities that he varied from day to day, just as he had in Tangmere: push-ups, squats, jumps, crunches, running on the spot. If nothing else, it was a relief to be physically active. It took him out to the fresh air and gave a form to his days, shook off the

149

staleness and made him feel he was doing something practical and useful rather than brooding on this enforced waiting game or trying to distract himself with Marie's little library.

He took to running along the perimeter of her pasture. In better times, it would have been grazing land, but now the grass and wild flowers grew freely. As he ran, he always kept a wary eye on the lanes and surrounding roads in case any German vehicle appeared.

One evening, he finished his run as dusk was beginning to fall. The moon had returned; tonight it was a plump oval. He watched it rise as he ran. He detoured to the ruined graveyard to cool down. As he came to a halt and tried to catch his breath, he glimpsed a flicker of movement somewhere up ahead and heard voices talking quietly. He stepped quickly behind the ancient yew tree. Its girth was more than enough to conceal him.

Two men were absorbed in some task among the ruins of the church. One was standing upright, the other was crouching down. They were looking at something on the ground. He could not make out what the object of their attention was; the remains of one of the walls blocked it from his view.

Then something seemed to move on the stonework at the base of the church tower. It moved again, and he saw that it was a thin cable or wire. It ran from ground level, where it was just visible against the grey stones, and disappeared inside the tower.

He looked up to the top of the tower. A man was peering out from a narrow window at its highest level, just below where the spire began. The tower was severely damaged; the stairs within it were sure to be unsafe. The man had taken a risk to get where he was – and would repeat that risk when he descended. The entire tower and spire could come down on him. What was important enough to justify such a risk?

All at once, Archie understood what he was seeing. The wire was an aerial, an antenna. The object on the ground in the ruins of the church, the thing he could not see, must be a wireless transceiver – battery powered. The man in the tower was looking for a way to fix the end of the aerial in place. If he succeeded, the portion at ground level could be coiled up and hidden away inside the tower until it was needed.

Archie decided he had seen enough – and certainly more than he was meant to see. It was time for him to leave. He stepped away from the tree, turning to retrace his steps. And found himself confronted by two men. The sweat from his run was suddenly chill on his skin.

They looked like ordinary working men. But the tools of their particular trade were the submachine guns cradled casually in their arms.

'You're the English airman,' said the older of the two. It was simply an observation; there was no threat in his voice. He spoke around a skinny unlit cigarette at the corner of his mouth.

Archie nodded. He looked more closely at the men's weapons. They were British Sten guns. They would have arrived in France by parachute drop. British guns, delivered by a British aircraft. So the men – not just these two, but presumably the other three as well – were Resistance.

Simone's comrades.

The man lit the skinny cigarette.

'All this running about, Englishman – you need to be careful, it's asking for trouble. But I suppose it doesn't matter now. We were just about to come looking for you.'

Archie did not like the sound of that. Armed men looking for him? Even if they were Resistance.

But before he could say anything, a sudden noise made the three of them turn towards the church. The man had descended from the tower. Safely, but only just. Rubble tumbled after him as he jumped clear.

The racket covered the approach of the person who now joined the two armed men.

'I have news for you, Archie,' said Simone. 'And something else as well. This is yours. You can have it back now.'

She handed him his revolver.

Marie knew why Archie had begun exercising with such determination. She knew why he ran in her pasture like a wild man, sometimes wearing on his back an old rucksack of Heini's filled with bricks or stones from the ruined church. He was getting ready for when Simone would come to fetch him. He was preparing himself for his departure from Belville – his departure from *her*. However hard she had tried to dissuade him, all her efforts had come to nothing.

And now it seemed that the time she dreaded was here. She had seen the men arrive this evening while Archie was out on his run. She recognised them; they were Simone's comrades. All five of them were armed with submachine guns and pistols. Three of them went to one of the ruined cottages, and there they remained.

Like everyone else in Belville, she knew that some of the ruined cottages were used as hiding places for firearms, explosives and other equipment. Clearly an action or operation of some kind was under way. An operation such as spiriting someone away from here and to safety, perhaps. Someone like Archie.

While the three men busied themselves in the cottage, their two companions moved silently about the village as lookouts, sometimes taking cover in other abandoned cottages, sometimes crossing through the yards of inhabited dwellings. They asked permission of no one, and no one challenged them. People simply kept to their homes, their shutters closed, knowing that when the men's work was done – whatever that work was this evening – they would depart as unobtrusively as they had arrived.

The one inhabited dwelling the men did not disturb, the one yard they stayed away from, was hers. This was how things had always been. It was what Heinrich had promised her.

'Any time Simone's men come to Belville, they won't trouble you, meine Liebe,' he had explained a long time ago. 'Simone will always see to that. You don't need to worry. They'll do what they have to do, but Simone knows that her world and mine must not touch, they must never intersect.'

So it had always been and so it was this evening, even in Heini's absence.

After a time, the three men emerged from the ruined cottage. One of them was carrying a small suitcase. Small but heavy, a dead weight: plainly it held something a lot more substantial than a few bits of clothing.

They came towards her cottage and she moved away from the window, preferring not to be seen. But as they reached the graveyard, they turned towards the ruined church. Their two guardians followed, still watching all around, then they disappeared into the graveyard.

The three men with the suitcase entered the church. They set the suitcase on the ground. One of them crouched down and seemed to be opening it, but it was out of her sight now and she could not see what it contained. Then, to her astonishment, one of the men began climbing inside the tower. Below him trailed a wire of some kind. Higher and higher he went.

Across her pasture, she saw Archie returning. Her head filled with stupid ideas – the most insane ideas, but she could not stop them: perhaps she could keep him from encountering the men; perhaps if she did that, they would leave without him. Stupid, stupid ideas.

He had no rucksack this evening, there were no bricks to slow him down, and almost before she knew it, he had passed her cottage and yard without glancing in her direction, his entire attention focused on his running, and went straight to the graveyard.

Then he stopped abruptly and she knew he had seen the men in the church.

She saw the two armed guardians confront him. She saw Simone join them.

And knew that any hope of Archie's departure being prevented or delayed was lost.

Archie took the revolver from Simone.

'So you no longer believe I'm a German spy.'

'I never said you were – only that there was a risk you might be.'

'And what persuades you I'm not?'

'We contacted London, London contacted your squadron. They confirmed the identity details you gave me. They also confirmed that a man using the name Loïc Boiteux was your passenger. Not his real name, as it turns out. They were regretful to learn of his fate. They'll inform his family.'

'There were others that night – the local agent and his group, the passengers I delivered. What became of them?'

She shook her head. She wanted no digressions. 'I don't know. You get the green light from London and your squadron, but I needed more than that.'

'What do you mean?'

'The Boche could have obtained your details from the real pilot – under torture if necessary. They would have had Loïc Boiteux's ID card in their possession just as you did. So these things alone weren't enough for us – we must always be careful; the lives of our people are at stake. Fortunately, I was able to do some other checks of my own. They took a little longer. That's why you had to wait.'

'What other checks?'

'Do you remember what I told you about your arrival in Belville, that you were observed from the moment you got here?'

'Of course.'

'Well, you were also observed as you made your way here – in fact, more or less from when you left your crashed aircraft.'

'Observed by whom?'

'People in their farms and homes. People who were awake because of the explosion. Awake and watching, because who goes back to their bed after something like that? They saw you as you entered or left their land or their neighbour's. They put two and two together – an explosion, possibly a crashed aircraft, and now here was someone behaving suspiciously in the middle of the night, trying to keep out of sight. People tell us when something's out of the ordinary. We followed up on the reports until we knew exactly where you'd been seen. From that, I was able to reconstruct your journey and its many detours. If you were a Boche spy trying to infiltrate our network, you wouldn't have made such a journey with all those time-consuming detours. You could have gone to any of the homes or farms you passed and claimed to be from the crashed aircraft.'

'Or I could have come directly to Belville if I suspected there was a Resistance network here.'

'Correct. No need for any detours.'

'So the people who observed me were Resistance?'

'No, just ordinary people. There are many ways to oppose the Boche. Some people take up arms, as my comrades and I have done, but many more are just like the people of Belville – they keep their eyes and ears open. They're *our* eyes and ears. That's also how we knew what happened at the crash site – the discovery of the dead man and the search for you that was put in hand.'

'And it's how you knew about Heinrich's involvement in the search. And the Gestapo officer.'

'Once again, information that came from ordinary people, our eyes and ears. Ordinary people that the Boche in their arrogance don't even notice, as if those people don't exist. But they do exist. They're there, always there, watching the Boche all the time.'

'So what happens now?'

'It seems you're an important man, Archie. Your squadron wants you back with all possible urgency. That's how the reply from London put it, those were their words – all possible urgency.'

'Good. So how quickly can it be done?'

She turned to look at the men working in the ruins of the church. Archie followed her gaze. The light was fading, but he could see that the antenna had now been connected to the object on the ground, confirming that it was indeed a transceiver. So this was her link with London.

She turned back to him.

'I said I would make the necessary arrangements. That's now been done. You'll be leaving France the same way you came – by Lysander. All we need is the recognition letters for the pick-up. London hasn't released them yet. That's why we've set up the transceiver.'

After all the waiting, a pick-up by Lysander was the best possible news: it meant no lengthy overland trek with the dangers that would entail. And he would be home all the sooner – all possible urgency, just as London had said.

But the good news came with a sting. Simone had paused. He realised she was preparing him for her next words.

'The pick-up will be tonight, Archie. You're leaving us tonight. At midnight.'

This was a shock. He tried to take it in: the implications for him, the implications for Marie.

Simone was watching him. Now was the time for her

to twist the knife. Marie would be rid of him and Simone need no longer fret.

But she did not twist the knife.

'Marie doesn't know,' she said quietly. 'I thought you might want to be the one to tell her.'

'Thank you. It won't be easy.'

'Young love, Archie. It's never easy.'

He made no reply. Once again, she was assuming more than she had any right to do. But it did not matter now. And there were other priorities that had to be dealt with before breaking the news to Marie.

'Simone, do you or your comrades have any experience with Lysander pick-ups?'

'We don't need any. We have you.'

'In terms of location, we should –'

'Location is already settled. We can't risk transmitting coordinates in case the Boche pick up the transmission, so we'll use the same location as a successful arms drop of a few months ago – a drop by parachute. That operation's code name was all that London needed for tonight. They've confirmed their understanding.'

An arms drop. Perhaps the source of the Sten guns that Simone's comrades were carrying.

'And where was that drop?'

She nodded in the direction of Marie's pasture.

It could hardly be better. Using an already established and proven location was standard practice – and essential if there was no time to find a new one nor the means by which to communicate it safely as in this case, and when there was no dedicated local agent on the ground to handle the logistics. And he himself could not have chosen a better spot for a Lysander operation than Marie's pasture – he knew it was solid ground with no mud or obstacles within the field and no dangerous cable lines in the way, a site that would be highly visible to an approaching aircraft, with the ruins of the church a useful landmark. The absence of any main roads, with only lanes and narrow routes départementales instead, would make it almost impossible for the Germans to pounce suddenly or mount an ambush. If they did attempt anything, the people of Belville would see their every move; he was confident of that now.

And the moon? He glanced up at the evening sky. The moon was bright. Provided it remained unobscured by any cloud, it would be his friend again.

Everything was set fair.

Under his instructions, Simone's men fetched four flashlights and short poles on which to mount three of them. He paced out the flarepath, indicating where each pole should be positioned, and made sure they were all hammered securely in place and the flashlights firmly attached at the correct angle. It was a calm evening with hardly a breath of wind, but his time here had taught him that the wind sometimes picked up as the night wore on. The prevailing direction was from the west, so he orientated the flarepath accordingly.

Simone seemed impressed by how quickly the preparations were made, with no hesitations or changes along the way. She did not know how often he had paced out the pasture in his mind, allowing his imagination free rein for what he had never for one moment believed could actually happen. It had only ever been wishful thinking, nothing more than that, something to keep his spirits up in those days and weeks of waiting. And yet it was the very thing that was now happening.

It was time for him to go to Marie.

Marie had watched as night fell and Archie worked in the pasture with Simone's men, doing something that involved wooden poles and flashlights. Sometimes he paced back and forth as if he was measuring distances, other times he and the men seemed to be assessing the solidity of the ground itself, stamping their feet as they wandered about. She had no idea what they were planning, but she knew well enough what it signified. Archie was leaving.

Now the work seemed to be done, the flashlights were extinguished and there was only the pale moonlight over the pasture. Archie spoke for a time with Simone, both of them glancing occasionally towards Marie's cottage. They were talking about her.

She got on with preparing dinner. It was to be a special dinner; that had been her plan. Food supplies these days were not what they had been when Heini was here with her, but from time to time she would barter with a neighbour, trading a bottle or two of Heinrich's wine or some cigarettes for a few eggs or a piece of chicken. Today she had struck good fortune and there would be beef for dinner. All afternoon she had been anticipating the moment when she would put plates on the table and see surprise and pleasure in Archie's face. That was all she ever wanted, all the reward she ever hoped for: to know that she was giving him pleasure.

But now tonight's meal – if he was still here to share it – would be the last she would ever put before him, the last they would have together.

No word of warning. He would be gone. She had known it would happen, but reality was hard.

She heard his footstep behind her as he entered the cottage. She did not turn to him, did not raise her head. She continued chopping vegetables.

'Marie –'

At the sound of his voice, her resolve broke. The tears were coming and she would not allow that. She dropped the knife onto the chopping board and made for the door. He moved to block her way, but she ducked her head, refusing to meet his gaze, and he stood aside.

Outside, the night received her. Nothing stirred in the moonlight, as though all Belville had been abandoned. She was alone; he was not following her. She listened for his footstep again, but the only sounds were the rustle of insects and the mournful whisper of the ocean. Simone and the armed men were nowhere to be seen, for which she was thankful, for she did not want their company, much less Simone's scolding. They were probably in the ruined cottage they had used earlier – waiting now for whatever was to happen that would take Archie away from her.

Whatever that was, she did not want to know. She did not want to see.

The tears burst forth. She ran into the night.

Archie waited a while before following her outside. Best to give her some space, time to cool off. He assumed he would find her waiting for him to join her. She was upset because he was leaving, he understood that, and she might well be angry – but she would be there, waiting for him.

But she was not there. He went a distance along the lane. No sign of her. He looked in her greenhouse. Not there either. She was being foolish, and tonight of all nights was not the night for that. Her bicycle was still here; she could not have gone far. He checked the yard, all the way to the far end, and looked in the barn, going right inside to peer through the darkness. He went to the ruins of the church and the graveyard, to the grave of her mother and father. Again, no sign of her. He returned to the cottage – perhaps she had slipped back in while he was outside. But she had not, and the half-prepared meal was exactly as she had left it. He went to the pasture in case she had become curious about what he was doing there with Simone's men. Perhaps he should have asked her permission to use the pasture – in fact, perhaps as the very first thing, he should have gone to her to break the news that he was leaving. But he had barged ahead like an idiot, thinking only of himself and his own plans, swept away by his excitement to be leaving at last, and completely neglecting Marie.

Too late now for him to realise that. But whatever the rights and wrongs, the simple fact was that she had gone. And it seemed that she did not want to be found.

Simone appeared as he was returning from the pasture. One look at him told her something was amiss.

He explained. At first, she was merely amused.

'You argued?'

He shook his head. 'I didn't have a chance to say anything. She just walked out. We didn't speak a word. Not a word.'

'Ah, the worst kind of argument – the silent kind. But she'll come back in her own time. Don't worry.'

'Easy for you to say. I must find her. We must find her.'

She was no longer amused. 'We must, Archie? We must? What would you have us do? Search the village, scour the countryside? Go from door to door looking for her? Should we tell London its aircraft must wait until you find your lover and kiss her farewell?'

'She's not my lover. We're not lovers.'

'So you say. Whatever you are, you're the one who reminded me she's an adult, not a child. She has every right to go off by herself if she wishes. And we don't go chasing after her.'

'Is this how Belville looks after its own?'

'Belville lets people make their own decisions.'

'Provided those decisions suit you and your comrades, of course. Like allowing Marie to be with Heinrich because that suited you. Maybe you even encouraged her. Did you do that, Simone? Did you use her after her parents died, did you push her into Heinrich's arms? Did you use him too?'

As soon as the words left his mouth, he knew he had gone too far. Simone's hand whipped viciously across his face, then back again, striking each cheek in turn, snapping his head from side to side with the force of each blow. She was physically strong, and the blows were delivered with all the power she could pack into them. There was nothing ladylike about them. They were painful enough in their own right, but their effect was

164

magnified by the jolts of pain in his head wound.

He could not have said which of them, himself or Simone, was the more shocked. They stood frozen, staring at one another. Neither of them spoke of the blows or the words that had provoked them; and somehow he knew with certainty that if ever they met again, neither of them would speak of this moment.

His cheeks stung. He willed himself not to touch them. He heard the slow, deep breath she inhaled as she calmed herself.

'Listen to me, Archie. I told you to be careful with Marie. I warned you not to hurt her; I warned you she was fragile. Who knows where she's gone, or why. Who knows whether she'll return for that farewell kiss. All we know is this: whatever your feelings for her, it's time to put them aside. The same goes for Marie. If she doesn't know that already, she'll learn it soon enough – however painfully. So we won't go looking for her. Are we settled on that? We'll concentrate on what we have to do tonight.'

He knew she was right – just as she was right in something else she had once said and even he himself had always accepted: that he was here today, gone tomorrow.

And now tomorrow had come.

The waiting was not easy – different in kind from the waiting of his time here. In the first place, it was the waiting of anticipation sharpened by anxiety: in these last hours, these last minutes, could something go wrong, had some crucial detail been overlooked?

And above all else, the waiting was coloured by Marie's absence. Always, when he had thought about this moment, the moment when he would have to part from her, he had hoped there would be time for them to approach it in some way that would allow for their feelings for each other, however those feelings might be defined. But instead, it had come rushing upon them with no warning – and now, thanks to his own stupidity, she was not here for that moment.

He could not bring himself to enter the cottage or wait there: too many reminders of their too-brief life together. He stepped into her little greenhouse and left the .38 revolver where she would find it: hardly a romantic parting gift, but perhaps a practical one.

Then he wandered restlessly around the pasture, telling himself it was wise to remain there in case the Lysander was early – but knowing full well that his real reason was so that he would see Marie if she showed up anywhere. But she never did.

He was the first to hear the aircraft. The sound began as a faint drone, as soft as the murmur of the distant surf, and initially barely distinguishable from it. But his ear was attuned to that familiar sound and he easily separated it out. He raised an arm to alert Simone and the others, who by then had positioned themselves at points around or in the pasture: two of the men and Simone as lookouts, and each of the other three men responsible for one of the flarepath flashlights.

Suddenly, the Lysander was there, swooping directly overhead, a black silhouette that shot across the broad oval of the moon and chased its own moonlight shadow along the pasture. His heart leapt at the sight. He knew every move the pilot was making, every control he was touching, every instrument he was monitoring.

The aircraft completed its first pass over the landing zone, the pilot looking for anything there or in the wider area that suggested danger, then it looped back for a second check. As it approached again, Archie flashed his recognition letter for the operation, the letter provided by London: dot–dash–dot for R. The pilot responded immediately and correctly: dash–dash–dot–dot for Z. Archie called out to Simone and her men over the roar of the aircraft. The three flashlights marking the flarepath came to life: an inverted capital letter L. His heart leapt again. How he had missed all this.

Seconds later, the Lysander was safely down and taxiing into position ready for take-off. A perfect landing. Textbook.

He sprinted across the pasture, reaching the Lysander even before it had rolled to a stop.

'Hey there!' called the pilot. 'There's a beer waiting for you in Tangmere!'

No one was being dropped off. There was no luggage to load or unload. As soon as Archie was aboard, the aircraft was accelerating along the flarepath for take-off. It had been on the ground for little more than a minute.

There was time only to raise an arm in farewell to Simone and her comrades, then the Lysander climbed into the night sky.

Archie took a last look down. His breath caught in his throat. A solitary figure stood motionless in the furthest corner of the graveyard, beside one of the hideous family mausoleums. The bronze door was wide open. It was the tomb in which he had been hidden. In the moonlight, the statuary cast its chill shadow over the small, slight figure, but he knew who it was. He knew that angel of flesh and blood.

Then the aircraft banked sharply and he lost sight of her.

Some days were better than others for Heinrich.

There were the days when he could shuffle unaided all the way from the door of the interrogation room to the wooden chair at the centre of the room – instead of having to be dragged there by the guards or carried by the giant corporal. He could only move at a snail's pace and was prone to falling over, but he still considered it a significant achievement. It meant that Klemt was not winning.

There were the days when the swelling around his right eye reduced enough for the eye to open slightly. The left eye was completely blind now and he might never regain its use, but it was wonderful to be able to discern daylight with the right eye as his guards took him to the interrogation room, wonderful to catch a glimpse of the sky, of clouds, of birds on the wing.

But other days – many days and in the majority, a growing majority – were not so good. These were days when fear threatened to overwhelm him. Not fear of death, for that would be a release, a cessation – though not what he wished for – but fear of what was being done to his body, fear of what he might have to live with, if he lived. What if he lost the sight in his surviving eye, leaving him totally blind?

Then there was the matter of his hands. All the fingers and the thumb of his right hand had been broken. He had no way to reset the bones. So even if they knitted together, they might do so wrongly and the hand might be useless. And what if Klemt instructed the corporal to smash the left hand as well?

He had been drowned several times. The corporal strapped him to a board and plunged him into the tank, keeping him submerged until Heinrich could no longer

168

hold his breath and filled his lungs with water. He blacked out and knew no more until the corporal revived him, pressing his considerable weight on Heinrich's chest to expel the water. From the constant pain he now suffered in his chest, he was sure the man had cracked several of his ribs. But above all, the drowning was terrifying because his brain was being denied oxygen. How many such episodes would it take before his brain was damaged permanently?

He was now unable to carry and empty his latrine bucket. The guards refused to do it for him. The bucket overflowed. It stank worse than ever. The cell stank. He stank. He was being reduced to the most primitive degree to which a human being could fall.

His nose was broken. The bone moved freely from side to side. Both his ears were swollen; he could not always hear properly. Sometimes he passed blood, which he assumed was the result of internal injuries inflicted by the corporal's assaults and the kickings that the guards doled out. The doctor who checked him over at the beginning of each day to ensure he was up to what lay ahead – because he would be no use to Klemt dead – ignored him when he asked about this. So presumably, however bad the damage, he was expected to last long enough for Klemt to get what he wanted out of him.

But Heinrich knew better than that. Klemt would get nothing out of him.

'Nothing!' he promised himself.

As for the interrogation sessions themselves and Klemt's working method, sometimes the Gestapo man was the epitome of reasonableness, a friend who was trying to help him out.

'These people are taking advantage of you, Hauser.

Can't you see that?'

'I'm having difficulty seeing anything at the moment, Herr Major. What people do you have in mind?'

'Senior Wehrmacht officers – the people who make you supply them with illicit goods that belong by rights to the Reich. People like your Major Naumann. They get you to take all the risks. There's plenty for them to enjoy as conquerors here in France; they live the good life, but for some of them it's never enough. There's a certain type that always want more. It's because of them that black markets exist. And these black markets undermine the Reich.'

'A scandal, Herr Major.'

'Black markets dishonour our noble cause. They steal what belongs to Germany. I want to help you, Hauser. I don't think you're the kind of man who would deliberately go against Reichsmarschall Göring's orders. This is about corruption in the Wehrmacht at the highest levels. It's my view that what has happened here is that people like Naumann put temptation in your way, and that's why you got yourself involved in their schemes. You simply made a mistake, that's all. Anyone can make a mistake.'

'Not me, Herr Major. I didn't. But you're right that some people do make mistakes. And in this instance, it's you who are mistaken.'

'Look, Hauser – it may interest you to know that I've arrested Naumann. It's only a matter of time before I get a full confession from him. But if you tell me everything now, I can ensure that you'll be dealt with leniently.'

'But how can I tell you everything? What is there to tell?'

'Give me the names of everyone who buys from you.

Give me the names of your suppliers, because they're the real criminals here; they're the ones who are dishonouring the Reich. Tell me where you store your stocks of goods. What do you use – is there a warehouse somewhere, a secret bunker? Hand everything over and I'll make sure your cooperation is rewarded.'

'With respect, Herr Major, I've never sold anything to Major Naumann. Actually, I've never sold anything to anyone. You saw for yourself – the only goods I had were those few bottles of wine. It was my intention to sell them, I admit, but you were too clever for me; you caught me out before I could do so. And as I told you, I obtained them through a French civilian whose identity I never knew.'

Since the bottles of wine had been planted, this was of course nonsense, and they both knew it. But Klemt the good friend, the reasonable man, heard him out, sighed and shook his head in disappointment, then nodded for the corporal to begin again with his fists or the bludgeon.

Then there was the Klemt who was no friend of Heinrich's, who lost all patience, who shrieked and screeched at him like a demented demon, spit flying from his thin lips. Sometimes it was merely an act, but at other times Heinrich could see that the Gestapo man had genuinely lost control. On occasion, this uncontrolled Klemt wielded the rubber bludgeon himself.

Against these tribulations, Heinrich's strategy for dealing with the Gestapo man was first to deny everything.

'Major Naumann can't tell you anything, Herr Major, because there's nothing for him to tell – not about me, anyway.'

Then, for variety, he wove a tapestry of confusion.

'What about the wine and cognac *you* bought from me, Herr Major? Does that count as part of my crime?'

'What are you talking about? I bought nothing from you.'

'Don't you remember? There's a witness, someone who saw the transaction, and he claims to remember it well enough.'

'That's impossible. There was no transaction, so there's no witness.'

'But there is. That's the truth. Why not bring him in for questioning? You really should do that. Don't just take my word for it. Hear for yourself what he has to say.'

'I'm not taking your word. Why would I waste my time bringing anyone in? I'll get all the truth I need from you. There is no witness, I said. There can't be.'

'Fine, if you want to believe that. But who knows how many people he may have told already. Who knows how many they in turn may be telling. Before you know it, you'll be the one under investigation.'

'That's ridiculous. Who is this witness?'

'His name's Mannstein. Oberleutnant Mannstein. A Bavarian. Looks a bit like a tortoise. Come to think of it, you know him – he's your informant, isn't he? You should never have trusted him, Herr Major – he's turned on you. Typical Bavarian.'

Anger darkened Klemt's bony features. But clearly the thought of what Mannstein might be saying behind his back was a troubling one, for after a couple of days of Heinrich's claims, he disclosed that the Bavarian had been arrested.

'I've interrogated him, Hauser, and naturally he denies your accusation. How could he do otherwise, since what you said was a pack of lies?'

'Ach, of course he denies it, Herr Major – but with respect, whether or not our transaction took place is beside the point. What matters is what he was saying about you. On that, I stand by what I said. Tell your corporal to put more effort into his work with him. Maybe he's losing his touch.'

Next, Heinrich shifted his ground. He blamed the interrogation – and therefore, by implication, the interrogator, Klemt himself, that renowned and expert practitioner – for yielding nothing but false information.

'You went fishing, Herr Major, but you've caught nothing. I'm afraid all you've done is dredge up an old boot or two.'

Heinrich's jaw was swollen, possibly dislocated, he thought he might be losing another tooth to the corporal's most recent ministrations, and his words were garbled. Garbled but laced with all the defiance he could muster. The corporal flexed a fist, ready to strike again. Klemt held up a hand, restraining him.

'What are you talking about, Hauser? What does fishing have to do with anything? You're rambling. Are you delirious?'

'No, Herr Major. I'm telling you that I retract my original confession. I know you planted those bottles of wine in that cottage – at any rate, your driver did. The confession I made that day, I've stuck to it so far only because I hoped your corporal here might stop beating me. You see, that's the trouble with violence as an interrogation technique.'

'Violence? What violence?'

Klemt lowered his hand and nodded at the corporal. The fist landed. The tooth flew out.

173

Day after day, the interrogation continued, getting Klemt nowhere. The page of his writing pad with the start date of Heinrich's interrogation remained empty of any other content. At the end of each session, the Gestapo man put away his pen and the pad, the corporal rolled down his sleeves and grinned at Heinrich, and Heinrich was returned to his stinking cell. If his right eye was working, he gazed up at the rectangle of sky beyond the barred window and watched birds in the scruffy branches of the pine tree. He went through his mental checklist of his injuries and assessed how much worse he was than the day before. Sometimes he totted up his small victories, if there were any that day – a look of despair on Klemt's death's-head face or a lie by Heinrich that had sent the Gestapo man scurrying down some useless side road.

It was clear that Klemt was a fool, despite his reputation. What had prompted his investigation of Naumann's Kommandantur was nothing more than his obsession with black markets and their drain on what the Reich was plundering from France. He had no interest in partisan or Resistance operations, nor even in hunting down the enemy airman, a quarry by now apparently forgotten and never mentioned by Klemt. The only spy that interested him was his own informant, Mannstein, and the accusations Heinrich made against the Bavarian.

Above all, nothing led Klemt towards that other matter, the deepest secret of all. The secret that only Heinrich knew.

And so, when he was flung back into his cell at the end of each day, he dragged himself over to the thin mattress, adding fresh bloodstains to its pattern as he lay listening to the sounds of the world outside while it settled into evening. His body broken but his spirit stubbornly intact, he slipped into the merciful escape of sleep, hoping for nothing more than to dream of Marie.

The dreams came and she was there. But so, always, was the Engländer.

Archie had thought he would go straight back to 161 Squadron and his operational duties in Tangmere. Not so. Instead, he was shunted off to a large country mansion somewhere west of London, deep among the leafy lanes of the county of Berkshire. The echoing hall with its grand staircase recalled a more refined era before the Air Ministry had got its hands on the place. Now armed men in uniform kept watch among the avenues of rhododendrons in the surrounding parkland. Archie was the only house guest.

For almost two days, he was debriefed by a man who introduced himself as Mr Tyler and a woman who called herself Miss Bryant. No first names. No indication of how they fitted into things beyond a vague reference to being civil servants.

'Of a very lowly order,' added Mr Tyler, the older of the two.

They both wore civilian clothing and were clearly from one of the undercover or intelligence services – there was no shortage to choose from. Archie did not believe for one second that their names were Tyler and Bryant, and he could tell that they knew he did not believe it, nor was he expected to – but all three of them played along with the fiction.

Mr Tyler and Miss Bryant wanted every detail of what had happened to him in France – *every* detail, however small.

'From the very beginning,' said Mr Tyler.

'Yes, chronologically – we find that's usually the best way,' said Miss Bryant.

'Usually? So this debrief is normal procedure?'

Reassuring smiles. 'Oh yes. Perfectly normal. Under the circumstances. It's not like a debrief after a standard operation. Much greater depth, you see. All the details.'

'Circumstances? What circumstances?'

An apologetic dip of Miss Bryant's neatly coiffured head. 'You've been in enemy-held territory for quite some time.'

'Are you implying I might have been turned?'

Mr Tyler handled that one. 'Not implying anything, my dear fellow. Not our *place* to imply anything. Let's press on, shall we?'

Their pens scratched busily as Archie described the ambush in agent Armand's field and the crash-landing on the way back to England. They wanted to know the geography and timing of these incidents as best he could remember them. He told them about Loïc's death and how he had used the unfortunate man's body as a decoy. They wanted to know about the journey to Belville. He told them about the wound to his head and his evasion of German patrols – which he later discovered were in fact not only regular patrols but also search parties specifically looking for him.

'How did you discover that?'

'Initially, from someone called Heinrich. Later, a woman called Simone confirmed it.'

Both heads snapped up from the notepads. 'Heinrich? That's a German name.'

'Because he was German. A Wehrmacht officer. He led one of the search parties.'

'I don't quite follow. Are you saying you had actual personal contact with this German officer – in fact, you were on first-name terms with him?'

'Personal contact, yes, if you want to call it that. First-name terms, no. We spoke only once, briefly, one short conversation, and I didn't address him by his first name. I have to call him Heinrich simply because I never knew his surname. I still don't. He captured me, then he helped to protect me.'

'Protected you? From whom?'

'From the Germans who were searching for me.'

'But he was one of them! You just said so. And how did he protect you? He captured you, you said.'

'Yes, he did, but that came later, not during the overnight search. He also protected me from a Gestapo officer who was investigating him.'

'Investigating him for what?'

'Dealing in contraband goods. Black market. I don't know any more about it than that.'

Mr Tyler and Miss Bryant were looking slightly lost. Miss Bryant studied her notes. 'You mentioned someone called Simone. Who was she?'

'She turned out to be the local French Resistance leader. It's thanks to her I'm here. She arranged my escape. Look – someone in London knows all this already.'

'Who in London?'

'Whoever approved Tangmere sending someone to fetch me. I don't know who that was.' He eyed Mr Tyler. 'Not my *place* to know that.'

Miss Bryant ploughed on. 'Did they know one another, this Simone and Heinrich?'

'Apparently so, though I never saw that for myself. I never saw them together. But Simone told me that she bought some of Heinrich's contraband goods from time to time.'

'But obviously this Heinrich didn't know she was in the Resistance?'

'Who can say? Belville is an unusual place. My

impression was that Heinrich spent much of his off-duty time there and that the villagers thought highly of him. There was a bombing raid –' He stopped himself. 'But that's another story.'

Mr Tyler and Miss Bryant looked at one another. By now, they probably thought he was deranged. Possibly turned, possibly deranged. Possibly both.

'Simone was very unimpressed by my escape kit.'

Concerned frowns. 'In what way?'

He told them about her criticism of the ID photographs. This set them scribbling furiously. Presumably this little nugget would be relayed and acted upon somewhere.

The more questions they fired at him, the more disjointed became his tale, involving jumps in time and large gaps that made Miss Bryant frown and led her to scratch out and revise some of what she had written. After a while, they seemed to realise it was their own fault; they had departed from Miss Bryant's chronological guidelines, so they took him back to his overnight trek from the crash site.

They wanted to know why he had chosen Belville as his destination. They were especially interested in his encounter with Marie.

'So you threw yourself on her mercy?'

'That's a rather dramatic way of putting it.'

'But in essence accurate, would you say?'

'I suppose so. In its way. It's not the expression I would choose to use.'

'How would you express it?'

'I asked her to help me, that's all. Those words, literally. In French, I'm fairly sure. It's all a bit of a blur now, actually. I wasn't entirely compos mentis.'

There – they could draw whatever conclusion they

liked from that. No doubt the pendulum would swing towards deranged.

'How did you know Marie wouldn't betray you?'

'I didn't. I wasn't in any condition to know anything by then. I lost consciousness, and when I came to, she took me in.'

'Took you into her home?'

'Yes. And treated my head wound. I stayed with her until my return to England.'

'You were living with her? In her home?'

'After Heinrich's arrest, yes. I stayed with her from then.'

'So Heinrich was arrested in the end? By the Gestapo?'

'By the Gestapo officer who was after him.'

'I see. Well, let's not deal with his arrest just yet. Tell us about Marie. Why do you think she helped you?'

'Why does any human being help another? She was that kind of person – she *is* that kind of person.' He thought for a moment. 'A good person.'

'She was risking her life, surely.'

'Yes. Which makes her a *very* good person in my book. She persuaded Heinrich to help protect me.'

'How was she able to do that?'

He took a while to answer. 'They were lovers.'

Another exchange of glances between Mr Tyler and Miss Bryant. It was Mr Tyler's turn to take refuge in his notes.

He cleared his throat. 'May I try to summarise? This young woman, Marie, takes you into her home at great risk to herself. She and her lover, a Wehrmacht officer who deals in contraband goods and is being investigated by the Gestapo, give you protection. This includes protection from the Gestapo. The woman called Simone is a Resistance leader. The Wehrmacht officer may or may not know this. He is arrested by the Gestapo. It is Simone who arranges your escape from France, from German-held territory. Indeed, it may be no exaggeration to conclude that you owe your life to these three people.'

'That's about the size of it. Especially the last bit, about owing them my life. There's no exaggeration there.'

They quizzed him about Belville itself. He provided a physical description of the place. Inevitably, this led to the question of how so much of the village had come to be damaged.

'A bombing raid,' he said. 'Belville was bombed. By us. In error, obviously.'

He repeated the account Simone had given him, including the deaths that had been caused, among them those of Marie's parents. And village children.

'The people of Belville must hate us,' sighed Miss Bryant.

'Actually, I saw no evidence of that.'

He described what Heinrich had done in the aftermath of the disaster. Miss Bryant looked up from her notes.

'So perhaps that explains why the villagers thought highly of him?'

'I suppose so.'

'Let's see. They had reason to hate us, their allies, but you say they didn't. The German called Heinrich was their enemy, a representative of the occupying power, yet they regarded him highly.'

'I told you – Belville is an unusual place.'

'And this disastrous bombing raid happened at Easter last year?'

'Shortly before.'

Miss Bryant and Mr Tyler added to their notes. They had enough information for someone somewhere to identify the ill-fated operation.

Eventually, Archie's account came to the day of Heinrich's arrest. Archie related the bare facts as he understood them but could provide no details, since he had not been witness to the event.

'So where is Heinrich now?'

'God knows. In a lot of trouble. Locked up somewhere dreadful, I imagine. Probably being tortured. He may even be dead by now, for all I know.'

'Forgive my saying so, but I have the definite impression that you'd be sorry if Heinrich, this German officer and therefore your enemy, is dead or in trouble.'

Archie looked directly at Mr Tyler, whose observation this was.

'Mr Tyler, make no mistake – if that were the case, I would be *very* sorry. Simone used to say that Heinrich was a good man. And as far as I'm concerned, he was. You may categorise him as an enemy, but I see him as a good man.'

Eyebrows were raised. There was silence for a few moments while the dust settled on this declaration. Miss Bryant was the first to return to the discussion.

'You explained that this was when you began living with Marie, this Wehrmacht officer's lover. After his arrest.'

'That's the second time you've used that term – living with her, living with Marie. I wouldn't call it that.'

'Why not?'

'It suggests something more than was the case.'

'What do you think it suggests?'

Again he took a while. 'It suggests we were lovers. It suggests that Marie went from being Heinrich's lover to being mine.'

'To be clear, then – are you saying you weren't lovers, you and Marie?'

'That's precisely what I'm saying.'

Miss Bryant was watching him closely. 'I must say, though, I do sense you were particularly fond of Marie. And still are, perhaps, even now.'

'Wouldn't you be fond of someone who saved your life – and risked their own in doing so?'

'I really can't say. I'd be grateful to them, of course – but that's not quite the same thing as being *fond* of them.'

He disliked the way in which she said that, how she managed to make *fond* sound like a dirty word. For a moment, he was back in Belville, and Marie, so light in his arms, was dancing and laughing with him in the warm evening air. Change of scene and he was watching her as she slept, her head on his shoulder, her eyelids flickering as she moved from dream to dream.

This foolish Bryant woman knew nothing, understood nothing. She had no right to drag his feelings through the muck of her unsavoury imagination.

None of which he said.

'Look here, Miss Bryant – we weren't lovers. End of story.'

The questioning went on. And on. Covering the same ground repeatedly, unearthing more and more detail each time. At the end of the first day, it was midnight before they let him get to bed. Then they began again the next morning, arriving in their little Morris car and starting on him even as he was trying to have breakfast. He gave up and pushed the plate aside, his appetite gone. He wondered what Marie would eat today. He wondered if Heinrich was still alive.

But during the afternoon of that second day, something changed. There was a telephone call for Miss Bryant. Until then, Archie had assumed that Mr Tyler was the senior partner. It seemed he was wrong. Judging from the fact that the call was for her, not him, and considering the exchange of glances that followed between the two of them, this show was very firmly Miss Bryant's.

She was gone only a few minutes. When she returned, she cast a quick glance at Mr Tyler, a glance that Archie could not interpret.

'I think we've covered all the ground we need,' she told Archie brightly. 'You've been most incredibly helpful. A car will collect you shortly and take you to Tangmere.'

It was all very sudden. Mr Tyler looked mystified but caught Archie looking at him and quickly restored his expression to its accustomed blandness. Miss Bryant shook Archie's hand. Mr Tyler shook his hand. They each thanked him, though neither of them said for what. He thanked them in return, though he could not for the life of him think for what. Miss Bryant suggested he might want to get some fresh air before his car arrived. Mr Tyler agreed that sounded like a capital idea: rain was forecast, best to step out before it arrived. In short, they all played the game to the end.

Archie took the hint about fresh air and was happy to oblige. He left them to pack their briefcases and hurried from the room, hoping never to set eyes on it again. But in the echoing hall with its grand staircase, he remembered that his jacket was still on the back of his chair. He turned back towards the room. He stopped outside the door when he heard Miss Bryant's voice. She was not happy.

'Basically, it's a total shambles – one of their very finest,' she was telling Mr Tyler. 'This debrief didn't happen.'

'I don't believe this.'

'Those are my orders. We're to hand over our notes, every scribble. We haven't been here, there was no debrief. We're to put from our minds everything we've heard over the last two days – because we didn't hear it. And before you ask – no, I don't know why.'

Nor did Archie. But at least Miss Bryant and Mr Tyler knew whose orders they were – or whose they appeared to be.

Which was more than Archie knew.

Marie was alone now.

She sat in her yard and watched the afternoon shadows lengthen. In the pasture, the wooden poles and flashlights had been taken away by Simone's men, but the grass still bore the tracks made by the wheels of the aircraft.

Archie was gone. First Heinrich and now Archie. Both had gone from her by their own will in one way or another – Heini by giving in to the Gestapo monster, Archie in order to return to war. Her little cottage had become a place of painful emptiness, where her only company was memories. Everything her gaze fell upon summoned up Heini or Archie, sometimes both of them. Everything she touched had been touched by them: the musty old books that had fascinated Archie, the chair by the hearth that Heini had favoured. Here was her bed where she and Heini had made love – and here was the bed where Archie had slept, where they had never made love. Nor ever would, now.

Being alone was not a difficulty for her. She had been alone before, after the death of Maman and Papa. Heini had come into her life then, had brought healing to her, but no one would come into her life this time. But that was fine; it was a simple fact and not a matter for self-pity. She had never been one to feel sorry for herself for long, and she had no intention of doing so now. She would get by, she would survive very well. Belville looked after its own.

Thus, her concern was not for herself. Her concern was for Heinrich. And only Heinrich. Not for Archie, because he was safe somewhere in England. Ah, England! It was a country of which she had only vague notions based on the things he had told her about – afternoon tea, cricket, kings and queens – but it was a

186

country that the Germans had not reached and did not control. Idealised and fanciful as her picture of England might be, she was confident that Archie was safe there – unless he had indeed rejoined the war, a foolish man pursuing his foolish idea of duty, in which case he had no one to blame but himself if he was in harm's way. She regretted the manner of their parting, which was her own childish fault, but it was his safety that mattered, and on that, her mind was as much at ease as it could be. His fate now was in his own hands.

And so, her thoughts focused on Heini. He had sacrificed himself for her. He had protected and saved Archie. So this need she had now, the need to know where he was and what was happening to him – what was being *done* to him, if he was even alive – the fact that she still cared about him and worried about him, was that any surprise?

'Seb, what's going on?'

Archie put the question to Seb Wetherick, his commanding officer. They were in the squadron office in Tangmere. Outside, a stiff breeze drove barrages of rain across the airfield.

'Depends what you're referring to,' came the reply. Seb continued packing tobacco into his pipe.

'I've just wasted two days being grilled by an unlikely pair from one of the undercover services – though they never admitted that, let alone which service – only to discover that our time together never happened. Officially speaking.'

'Ah, that.'

'You know about it, then?'

'I do. But let's hear your version. Then I'll tell you something far more interesting than any of that bureaucratic claptrap.' Seb glanced up from fiddling with the tobacco pouch. 'Welcome back, by the way. None the worse for wear after your spell in France, I trust? You certainly look in fine fettle – apart from that little bump on your head. I suppose the hair will grow back eventually. Most of it.'

Seb had been on a pick-up operation of his own in France when Archie arrived back in Tangmere. Thanks to that and Archie's sojourn in Berkshire, today was the first time their paths had crossed.

'As you say, none the worse,' Archie assured him. 'All I want now is to get back to work, the sooner the better. I'm saying my encounter with our undercover friends never happened because that's what I overheard them saying at the end.'

Seb grunted dismissively. 'The fact is, someone dropped a clanger. While you and I were both in the air for our respective reasons, someone in Air Ministry Intelligence issued the order that got you exiled to Berkshire. I requested the order be rescinded as soon as I found out, but it took a while for the message to get through. You should never have been debriefed by that Air Ministry pair – because somewhere in what you told them, there may be a particularly sensitive piece of information. Something that's the strict preserve of the Secret Intelligence Service, theirs and theirs alone, and they're guarding it jealously. These undercover people, they never seem to talk to one another, do they? Too busy keeping too many secrets. Air Ministry Intelligence should have been warned off; they should never have stuck their oar in. And there you have it.'

So now Archie knew what lay behind the telephone call that the perfectly coiffured Miss Bryant had taken. And he knew whose order had brought it about – it was Seb's.

'And by the way,' added Seb, 'I'm not at liberty to tell you what that particular secret is.'

'So I know something very secret, but I'm not allowed to know what it is. I know it, yet I don't know it.'

'Got it in one.'

'What a silly game of riddles.'

Seb tilted his head in agreement. He was serious now. 'Silly, no doubt – but a game of deadly importance. I'm sorry you were caught up in it.' He settled back in his chair and got the pipe going. 'Now, speaking of secrets, there is one little secret I *can* actually share with you. I said I'd tell you something interesting, did I not?'

'You did.'

Seb puffed on the pipe. 'Tomorrow is D-Day.'

He said it as matter-of-factly as if saying nothing more

significant than that they would have lunch together. A cloud of tobacco smoke drifted towards the ceiling before being drawn out through the open window. A couple of mechanics in heavy all-weather gear were staring morosely at one of the Lysanders lined up in the dispersal area. Archie watched them without really seeing them, his thoughts racing. He could feel his heart pumping the way it used to when he was running in Marie's pasture.

'Dear Lord, Seb – it's on? It's really on?'

'It's on.'

There were a hundred questions Archie wanted to ask and have answered. He settled for the one on which there had always been the most speculation, along with the date.

'Where?'

'The Normandy coast. As it happens, the main attack force and beach landings will be concentrated near where you've just come from.' Now a glint appeared in Seb's eyes. 'History is being written, Archie. The world has never seen anything like this – the sheer weight of numbers, of men and equipment, of ships and tanks and landing craft, of naval artillery, of air assault and air cover for the invasion force and landings. The airborne part of the operation is massive and will be crucial – bomber attacks, paratroopers, hundreds of gliders bringing men in. That phase starts tonight, many hours before the landings, and there'll be no let-up throughout the night. If Adolf knew what's coming at him, he'd be quaking in his lederhosen. Actually, he'd do more than quake, but let's not be coarse. At this stage, the only factor that could work against us is the weather.'

'And the forecast?'

'Not perfect but better than today, which was a

possibility until the last minute. And the moon is with us. Full moon.'

The moon. Always the moon, governing even this mighty undertaking.

'Also, it's an early-rising moon. It rises before sunset this evening and it'll be in the sky all night long. Couldn't be better for air operations.'

'What about the tides?'

Seb nodded. 'The moon favours us again – it gives us the tidal conditions we need. The first is a low tide at sunrise, to get men out of the landing craft and through the water and onto the beaches as quickly as possible. Also, so that the Germans' underwater beach obstacles are exposed. The demolition units will deal with as many of those as they can. They'll only have half an hour or so before the tide rises too high for them – less if the weather turns rough and the sea gets too choppy – and they'll be under enemy fire throughout.'

'Terrifying.'

'Yes, but we need that rising water so that the landing craft don't get stranded. The worst thing we could do is launch them on a falling tide – they'd be marooned for twelve hours. On the part of the coast where the main invasion force will land, a low tide at sunrise occurs only at new moon and full moon. The top brass wanted a spring or summer invasion to allow plenty of time to push the enemy back before autumn and winter. Preparations weren't complete in time for the May moon, so that's why it has to be June. Can't be any later.'

'What's our role, Seb? How do we contribute? We can't just sit on our hands while the course of the war is being decided. We should be writing some of that history you mentioned.'

'I couldn't agree more. But we'll have to hold our horses just a little longer – we won't be idle, but we'll wait until we know exactly where we're needed and where we can be of most use.' He poked at the bowl of the pipe. 'Looks like you got out of Normandy just in time. Things are going to get rather busy there.'

Archie thought it best to make no reply to that. He wondered if Seb would see the notes of the debrief that had never happened, written by Mr Tyler and Miss Bryant who were never there. If he did, he could decide for himself how Archie might be feeling about what was about to happen to Normandy. And Belville.

As Archie left the squadron office, the rain was easing off, allowing some blue sky through the clouds. The mechanics were starting to work on the Lysander. It would be some time yet before that early-rising moon appeared – the moon by which he and everyone else in 161 Squadron lived and worked and by which the lives of many thousands of men would be measured tonight and tomorrow.

It was the middle of the night, the small hours. Marie was in her bed but not asleep. The noise she was listening to was a low-pitched rumble, steady and persistent, neither gathering strength nor reducing, neither coming closer nor moving further away. There had been storms today, bringing heavy rain, but this was not the storms returning, this was not rolls of thunder.

It was the sound of aircraft engines. Not a buzz like the sound of the small aircraft that had come for Archie. Nor was it the sound of German fighter aircraft that regularly patrolled the skies over the coast, protecting the system of military defences that Heinrich called the Atlantic Wall. This was the deep drone of heavy aircraft. It was the sound of bombers, of many bombers, and they seemed to be concentrating their activity in one location.

Now she heard explosions. She felt the hairs rise on the nape of her neck. If bombs were falling, then the aircraft were surely not German bombers setting out on a raid against England. They were English aircraft, they were incoming, and that meant they were bombing the Germans. Either way, English or German, they meant death. She knew how bombers sowed death; she knew death was never confined to the intended targets. So German bombers or English, what was the difference?

The difference? Tonight that difference meant everything to her.

She climbed out of bed and went outside. After the storms, the sky was now crystal clear, crowded with stars. The moon was full and huge, bright enough to show every detail of the familiar scene around her – the neighbouring cottages in the lane, her yard and barn, the ruins of the church. The steady drone of the bombers was unchanged, louder now but only because she was out of doors. Bright flashes lit the horizon, bursting into life and then dimming, only to be brought to life again: yes, definitely bombs, and the cause of the explosions she was hearing. They seemed to be in the area of Caen and Ouistreham.

She hurried back indoors, dressed quickly, returned outside and mounted her bicycle, and set off along the lane. Here and there, people had left their beds and were standing outside in little groups, talking together in subdued tones and gazing at the horizon as she had done. Someone called out to her as she passed, but she pedalled on, avoiding puddles that might conceal potholes and wreck her bicycle. She was grateful for the moonlight.

On the road, she was stopped twice, but the checks the two patrols made were cursory. Tonight these were frightened boys, not fearless Reich fighters and occupiers. Heinrich would have been disappointed in them. He would have taken them to task or found a way to reassure them and bolster their courage. But tonight Heini was not here to do anything like that.

The leader of the first patrol snapped something at her in German. He was trying to look dour and in command, but he merely looked miserable and lost.

He saw from her lack of response that she had not understood, so switched to bad-tempered French.

'Here is a restricted zone. You are not permitted.'

'Yes, I am. I live in Belville and it's within the zone. You have my papers – see for yourself. My mother is ill. I have to fetch medicine for her from a doctor in the next village. It's within the zone too, so I can go there.'

The explosions and the drone of the bombers continued as she spoke.

'They're attacking Caen, aren't they?' she added.

'They're bombing Caen.'

He ignored her. His face was white in the moonlight. Sweat glistened on his cheeks. He jumped at the sound of a particularly loud explosion. The men behind him moved closer to their truck as though they wanted to board it and be off to somewhere safe. Their dogs whimpered.

'Is this the invasion?' she asked the trooper.

He thrust her papers back at her. He did not meet her gaze. 'You ask a stupid question. There is no invasion. Not tonight, not ever. Heil Hitler!'

The second patrol was more honest.

'We don't know what's happening. Fetch your mother's medicine and get home as soon as you can. And stay there.'

She promised she would, even though she knew it was a promise she would not be keeping.

She cycled on, remembering how the troopers in the first patrol had edged nervously towards their truck. If this was the invasion, where did they imagine would be safe?

She wondered how many of them would still be alive this time tomorrow.

It seemed to Heinrich that his tiny world, this concrete cell, was about to be bombed out of existence, and himself with it. The whole barracks block shook violently with every explosion as though it was in the grip of an earthquake. Sirens wailed, both here in the barracks and in the distance beyond, in Caen itself. He wondered where the bombs were falling, what their targets were. He hoped they were nowhere near Belville and Marie.

A series of massive blasts close together shook the ground. Cracks appeared in the ceiling and walls of the cell. Chunks of concrete began to crash to the floor, some of them large enough to crush his skull. There was no way to predict where the next fall would be; all he could do was press himself into a corner and hope for the best.

He wondered how many bombers were converging on the city; it sounded like hundreds. He could detect the cannon clatter and screech of dogfights – Luftwaffe fighters would be attacking the bombers while the bombers' fighter escort would be retaliating, trying to protect the bombers. There was the steady crackle of flak as the city's anti-aircraft batteries tried to bring the bombers down.

Running footsteps passed by outside his window, first in one direction, then back again, a frantic traffic bordering on panic. Orders were barked, only to be countermanded a minute later. There were curses and shouts, the clang and rattle of weaponry. And always the pounding and thud of the bombs. It was a man-made hell.

His thoughts turned to escape. At any moment, the barracks might be hit. He had to find a way out, otherwise he would die here. He limped painfully from his corner to inspect the wall in which the door was set. But no matter how much the concrete crumbled elsewhere, the area around the door remained stubbornly intact. All that the destruction was achieving was to raise filthy clouds of dust that clogged his nostrils and throat. If the falling concrete did not kill him, the dust would suffocate him – unless a bomb scored a direct hit on the barracks and his cell. So whatever the manner of his death, it seemed that he was destined to die here, tonight, buried in this concrete coffin.

As though preparing him for that death, the cell's single light bulb failed. It had burned constantly throughout his time here, and for that reason he loathed it. Until now. Now he regretted its loss. He would have to do his dying in darkness.

He limped back to his corner, leant against the wall and let himself slide to the floor. He tried to close his mind to what was happening. He lost track of time, had no idea how long he had been there, when he thought he heard a familiar sound, only just audible amid the cacophony of other noise. He remained very still, listening hard. The sound came again. He had not imagined it. The door was being unlocked and unbolted. Someone was entering the cell. But who? Who in this hell would bother to come for him? And why? Klemt would not be sending for him to be interrogated this time. The Gestapo man's priority would be his own survival. No, this time they were coming to dispose of him. That angered him. To die in a bombing raid was one thing – a matter of fate, of being in the wrong place at the wrong time, a simple case of a man's luck running out. A decent way for a soldier to die. But to be put to death like a diseased dog? There was injustice in that. Humiliation, insult. He would deny them that if he could. He would deny Klemt. He would not go meekly. He wondered how much strength was left in him. He would fight to his last breath. He would not make it easy for them.

A cigarette lighter flicked. A flame appeared. He struggled with his one eye to bring the doorway into focus. But the figure standing there was not one of his guards. It was the giant corporal, the brute whose fists and tender care had brought him to his present condition. So his torturer was to have the pleasure of finishing him off. That figured.

The corporal moved the lighter from side to side, searching the darkness for his victim.

'There you are,' he said cheerfully. 'Let's get you out of here. Your guards have gone. Klemt too, by the way. No surprise there. Rats always get out first.'

He hoisted Heinrich to his feet. But in the corridor, he did not take him towards the stairs and Klemt's interrogation room; instead, he turned left and took him out to the compound. He was practically carrying him, Heinrich's legs were so weak.

The bombing had stopped. The drone of heavy aircraft engines was fading to nothing. The anti-aircraft batteries were silent, although searchlights still swept the sky. Fighter aircraft still passed overhead, but Heinrich assumed they must be Luftwaffe alone. One after another, the sirens were winding down.

The night air after the foulness and choking concrete dust of his cell was a relief, but he could smell burning. He squinted at the chaotic scene to which the corporal had brought him. The only light was from the full moon and the flames rising from a wing of the barracks that had been flattened. Teams of troopers with fire hoses were struggling to extinguish the flames, while others were being assembled in squads in the compound, evidently to be trucked out from the barracks. Vehicles were lining up, waiting for them. Elsewhere, medical teams were at work. An eerie silence now reigned.

'You're a fugitive now,' the corporal said. 'Get used to that.' He chuckled. 'Unless you'd prefer me to take you back to that cell.' He chuckled again. 'No? I thought not.'

He indicated the squads of men in the compound. 'You see our comrades over there? There are reports of enemy paratroopers somewhere nearby. No idea where they've sprung from, but they'll have been waiting for the bombing to stop. These fine fellows of ours are being sent out to deal with them. No doubt they'll do a good job, but I can tell you we're going to need more than that, more than a few squads like these.'

'What do you mean?'

'Something big is going on, and tonight's bombing raid is only a part of it. There's more –'

He was interrupted by a loud crash. They both ducked.

'Not a bomb,' decided the corporal. 'Maybe one of our vehicles outside the barracks, its fuel tank. Or a building coming down.'

Heinrich looked at the sky. It was red with fire.

'There's more, you were saying. Like what?'

The corporal blew out a long breath as he organised his thoughts. 'Like pockets of fighting all the way to the Cotentin Peninsula. Like enemy gliders landing with hundreds of infantrymen and equipment in more locations than I can list. Like paratroopers appearing from nowhere – in Gonneville, near Cabourg and Houlgate. Like bombers sighted off the coast northwest of here, and warships as well – not just the Normandy coast but also off the Pas-de-Calais, according to naval radar. This isn't just the English – there are reports of Americans at Hiesville and Sainte-Mère-Église in the west. It's going to be a long night, my friend, with even longer days and nights to follow. And the bombers won't have finished with Caen. They'll be back.'

'You're saying this is the invasion.'

'Why else would the enemy invest men and firepower on such a scale? If it's not the invasion, it's a decoy – meaning that the real invasion is still knocking at our door, but just a different door, that's all. I'm no military strategist. I only know what I hear. Let's hope our generals know more than I do. Let's hope they're paying attention.'

'Why are you helping me?'

The corporal grinned. 'Why not? It wasn't personal, you know, what I had to do. It was just my duty. I had my orders, from Klemt. But I took it easy on you.'

'Did you?'

'Of course. Without Klemt knowing, of course. We do what we have to do, we do what we're ordered – but not always *exactly* what we're ordered. And you led Klemt a merry dance. I enjoyed that. Good for you. Well, it's all in the past now. Now we're just ordinary comrades. And I wouldn't leave a comrade to die. But listen – I have to go. You're on your own now and you're not in great shape. Can you stand by yourself? Let's see if you can walk a bit. That's the idea – take a few steps. What do you think – will you manage on your own? Can you see well enough?'

'Where is Klemt?'

'Don't know, don't care. In hell, where he belongs. It's what he deserves. You know the stories, of course?'

'What stories?'

The corporal gave him a sideways look. 'About Klemt.'

'I haven't heard any stories. I know nothing about Klemt. I didn't have a chance to find out anything before he arrested me.'

The corporal chuckled again. 'It's said he'll be one of Germany's richest men by the end of this war, whoever wins. He's a pirate. For years, he's been hunting down people like you, enterprising people with profitable commercial interests. He throws everything at them – interrogation, torture – until he breaks them and they turn everything over to him. He scoops it all up, gobbles the lot – cash, stocks of luxury goods, in some cases even fine art. The real beauty of it is, no one lives to tell the tale. A man like you – you've done all right for yourself, you've built up capital and resources, you've been setting yourself up nicely. Am I right? Yes. But you're just one man. How many men like you has Klemt arrested and sunk his fangs into here in France? Ten? Twenty? Maybe more? Well, try multiplying your success by ten or twenty and you'll have some idea of Klemt's piracy. Politicians start wars, soldiers fight them – poor ignorant bastards like you and me and our comrades over there in the compound – but it's the Klemts of this world who walk away with the spoils. Real pirate treasure. But look, I've got to go now. I don't plan to sit here waiting for an English bullet. What I've told you about Klemt – you didn't know any of this?'

Heinrich shook his head.

The corporal sighed. 'Like I said, dead men tell no tales. Your Wehrmacht major – what was his name? Naumann? – he died under interrogation at Klemt's hands. I had the feeling you had a soft spot for Naumann, so I'm sorry to bring you bad news. Apparently, Klemt got nothing out of him. And the Bavarian, Mannstein, he's dead too. I didn't think you cared much for him, so maybe you'll be shedding no tears there. They're both gone, and such is life. But don't blame their deaths on me. Klemt used another specialist instead of me.'

'Maybe I was lucky to have you.'

A final cheerful chuckle and a hearty clap on Heinrich's back that almost felled him, then the corporal lumbered off.

Marie kept an eye on the horizon as she cycled. She saw some of the bombers when they were picked out by the Germans' searchlight beams, she heard the crackle and roar of anti-aircraft guns, but as far as she could tell, no aircraft was shot down: no fireballs in the sky, no aircraft plunging to the ground.

She was certain now that it was Caen that was under attack. She was travelling east. Off to the southeast, on her right, lay Caen, and above it the port of Ouistreham. Heinrich had always said that the city and the port would be important targets when the invasion came, along with the canal that linked them. So if this really was the invasion, his prediction was right.

By the time she reached the village of Reviers, halfway to her destination, the bombing seemed to be over. She stopped outside the mairie to catch her breath before tackling the long ride out of the village. People had come out from their homes and gathered together to watch the sky, as her neighbours in Belville had done. The aircraft had withdrawn and there were no more explosions. The anti-aircraft guns were silent now, the searchlights still scanning the sky, finding nothing. But the bombers had left their mark: the horizon glowed with fire. Caen was burning. She pressed on, more urgently than ever.

She had never been to the Kommandantur before. All she had to guide her was Heini's description of its location. But once she got to Tailleville, the château was not difficult to find. It was well defended, standing in its own walled grounds on the outskirts of the village. The walls, of varying heights where they formed parts of outhouses, were topped with barbed wire; some had slots in which she thought she glimpsed the gleam of rifle barrels. So this was the place that had always demanded so much of her Heini – *too* much of him – like a jealous lover who was never satisfied. And in the end, it had taken him from her.

But for all its imposing presence and power, tonight the Kommandantur was in a state of alarm. Wehrmacht vehicles raced through the narrow streets around it, sounding their horns to clear her out of their way. The drivers swore at her as they tore past, their vehicles barely missing her, almost toppling her, splashing her blouse and skirt with mud. But their anger did not fool her: there was fear in the night air, just as palpable here as among the young troopers on the road. Fear so strong she could almost smell it, like male sweat.

When she came in sight of the château, she dismounted and walked the last hundred or so metres, wheeling her bicycle. Massive red banners with black swastikas hung from the building's brick façade. In place of entrance gates there was a Wehrmacht checkpoint with a barrier. Signs in French warned that the place was forbidden to civilians. There were German words on the signs as well, presumably saying the same thing. Sandbags were stacked the length of the château's frontage. Its wide grounds were disfigured by trenches and bunkers manned by troopers with machine guns.

She was stopped at the checkpoint by two armed guards. They levelled their rifles at her.

'Halt!' barked one.

'I've come to see Major Naumann.'

The men exchanged glances.

'Naumann? What do you want with him?'

'That's private, between the major and me.'

Another glance passed between the guards. Then one of them laughed. A coarse laugh. He stuck out his belly and rubbed it in a circular motion.

'A baby? You have his baby?'

The other man laughed with him and made an obscene gesture.

She knew she was blushing in embarrassment. 'Major Naumann will be angry if you don't tell him I'm here.'

'Angry? Naumann? You think so?'

There was more of their stupid laughter, then the first guard extended his hand and clicked his fingers.

'Your papers.'

She handed him her ID card. Unlike the patrols that had stopped her on the road, he examined it carefully, looking from her to the photograph and back again.

'Wait here.'

He kept the ID and strode off, picking his way around the trenches, and entered the château.

The minutes passed – at least ten, she reckoned, then twenty. Troopers and officers hurried past, along with a steady stream of vehicles coming and going. The guard was kept busy raising and lowering the barrier.

Eventually, two men emerged from the sandbagged entrance of the château. One of them was the guard who had taken her ID and gone to fetch Major Naumann.

She had never met Naumann. But she knew that the man accompanying the guard was not the Wehrmacht major. He was the Gestapo officer who had arrested Heinrich, the monster with greedy eyes.

She cursed her luck. She wanted no dealings with this monster. But there was nothing she could do. She could not leave now, could not simply turn away and flee. The guard had taken her ID and she needed it back. Besides, the Gestapo man must have examined it, so he knew who it was who had come looking for Major Naumann. And even if she fled, he knew where she could be found. She was trapped.

His thin lips formed a smile as he drew near.

'Ah, Marie, we meet again.' He dismissed the guard with a nod. 'Dear little Marie – you remember me, I hope?' He clicked his heels, bowed his head. 'Major Friedrich Klemt at your service. I recognised you at once, of course, as soon as I saw your photograph. How could I forget such a pretty face? Pretty name, pretty face – as pretty as a picture!'

He swayed slightly, and she realised he had been drinking.

'I am delighted to see you, naturally,' he continued. 'But you should not be here, even under normal circumstances. And tonight is not a normal night. Tonight is dangerous.'

'Because of the invasion, you mean. It's happening.'

Suddenly, she knew why he was drinking. He was afraid, as frightened as everyone else in this place. The alcohol was either to boost his courage or as an escape, a refuge. He drank as a coward.

'Invasion?' he said, as if speaking with a dim child. He shook his head. 'No, no, no. Where did you get such a foolish idea? A myth! Caen has come under attack, that is all. And only a minor attack. The city's defences are excellent. The attack has been successfully repelled, and I am informed that very little harm has been done. The enemy has achieved nothing. The city is quiet now, all is in order.'

He looked her up and down, taking his time, a leisurely examination. She knew it was not the muddy state of her clothing that occupied his thoughts. She fought to restrain the shudder that those blue eyes roused in her. Eyes as cold as marble even through the haze of alcohol.

He blinked, seeming to collect himself as his study of her ended. 'So. You have come here alone at this time of night? You have cycled all the way from Belville?'

'It's not that far.'

'There were checkpoints, surely?'

'One or two. They weren't a problem.'

'And you did this during a bombing raid? Such courage!'

'The bombs weren't close.'

'I salute your boldness of spirit. Well, as I have said, Caen is quiet now, but there is always the possibility of further enemy action – I would not wish you to be caught in it. It is unwise for you to be out and about.'

'I came here to speak with Major Naumann. I would like to do that.'

'So I have been informed. But why do you want to speak with him?'

'I want to ask him about Oberleutnant Heinrich Hauser. You may remember, you arrested him.'

The thin smile again. 'Certainly, I remember. What do you want to know? And why ask Major Naumann? Why not ask me?'

'Major Naumann is Heinrich's superior officer. And I didn't know you would be here.'

'Unfortunately, Major Naumann is not available. But you can ask me what you want to know. I will do my best to help.'

'I want to know where Oberleutnant Hauser is being held. Is he safe from the bombs?'

'Ah, I see. How touching that you should be concerned about him. Your concern is misplaced, you know – after all, he took advantage of your trust by using your home for his illegal activities. You deserve better than that.'

'But where is he being held, please? Is he in Caen? May I visit him? Will he be put on trial?'

'All these questions! Sadly, I know the answer to only some of them. He will indeed be put on trial, a military trial. I assure you it will be a fair trial, although you must bear in mind that he has already admitted his guilt. Unfortunately, it will not be possible for you to visit him. As for how he is, you can be sure he is being treated well. But where he is – that I do not know. After arresting him, I handed him over to the Wehrmacht authorities.'

She knew he was lying. But which parts of what he said were the lies? That he did not know Heini's whereabouts? That he had handed him over to someone else? That Heini was being treated well? That he would receive a fair trial?

Perhaps all of it was lies. But she could not allow herself to believe that. That would mean there was no hope.

He was looking at her again, as though he could see right through her mud-stained clothing.

'I have a suggestion,' he said. 'You should return to Belville now. Are you alone there in your little cottage? All alone?' He sighed. 'You should not be alone. As soon as possible, I will find out everything I can about Oberleutnant Hauser. You will be safe at home, knowing I am doing everything humanly possible. You can rely on me. A good idea, yes?'

Her flesh was crawling, but she muttered her

agreement. He handed her the identity card. But as she reached out for it, he suddenly clasped her hand, bent over it and kissed it, clicked his heels together, then looked up and smiled at her.

As she cycled away, she could feel his gaze following her, burning its way into her. She did not look back.

Caen had become a city of ghosts and rubble. The ghosts were the people who wandered lost through the destroyed streets. Most were French civilians, but Heinrich also saw the occasional Wehrmacht officer or ordinary trooper, stragglers who had been away from barracks when the bombing began and for whatever reason had failed to take cover. Some had been seriously wounded; some looked as though they had lost their wits, whether wounded or not. Some tried to attach themselves to him, seeking companionship. He shook them off, determined to keep his distance, even more determined that they should keep theirs. Broken and weak as his body was, half blind and limping, still he wanted no help from anyone and had none to offer. He was a fugitive, as the corporal had pointed out. He wanted no awkward questions, did not want to have to account for himself to anyone. He put his trust in himself and no one else. After all, it was how his life had always been: trusting no one.

Except Marie.

He came upon a dead Wehrmacht officer. Whatever had killed him had left no mark on him or his clothing. With difficulty, Heinrich stripped the greatcoat from him and put it on. It was hard work and sapped his strength, but now at least his own filthy condition was less immediately evident and less likely to attract unwanted attention. Besides, he was far from being the only wanderer covered in dust and dirt. He still stank, but who tonight would notice that when the stench of death was everywhere?

The dead Wehrmacht officer was armed. In death, he would have no more need of a weapon than of a greatcoat. Heinrich took the Luger pistol and a spare magazine.

He heard the roar of vehicles approaching at speed and hid himself in a bombed-out warehouse, limping as fast as he could to get there. A convoy of trucks rattled past, carrying heavy machine guns and squads of troopers – probably some of the men that he and the corporal had observed in the barracks compound. They were heading north, towards Ouistreham. Shortly afterwards, he heard bursts of machine-gun fire from that direction. So the corporal was right about the presence of enemy paratroopers. At first, the gunfire was sporadic, but soon it became continuous. Hard fighting was under way. Heinrich knew the area around Ouistreham and the canal. It was a network of sleepy rural neighbourhoods: Ranville, Amfreville, Bénouville. If that was where the fighting was concentrated, it suggested that the enemy was trying to take the bridges over the Orne river and the Caen canal.

He was about to leave the warehouse when he heard a noise. Something had moved in the darkness. Probably a rat. But the noise came again, the sound of something scuffling along the ground. Something large and slow. No rat could be that size.

He drew the Luger and cautiously edged his way towards the corner where he thought the sound was located. Even in the darkness of the warehouse, even with his limited eyesight, he recognised the bulky figure of the corporal. He was slumped against a wooden box filled with machine parts.

Heinrich crouched down beside him. The metallic smell of blood was unmistakable.

'What happened?' Heinrich asked him.

The corporal took a moment to focus on him. 'It's you? Is it you?'

'It's me. Tell me what happened.'

'French bastards. Three or four of them. Knifed me. In

the end, it wasn't an English bullet I had to watch out for.'

'I'll have a look at the wound.'

'Too many wounds, my friend. Too many knives, too many wounds. Save yourself the trouble. I'm done.' The corporal raised a fist – one of the mighty pair that Heinrich remembered all too well – and grasped Heinrich's arm. There was no strength in the grip. 'I got hold of a truck. Over there. It's yours now.'

The fist gestured weakly towards the far end of the warehouse, then fell to the ground.

Heinrich searched for a pulse. There was none.

He found the truck where the corporal had indicated. It was an Opel Blitz, a light open-backed vehicle smaller than a troop carrier. He would be driving half blind and would have to shift gear with the wrong hand, but the Opel would do the job that his exhausted and shattered body on its own could not do. It would get him out of Caen.

As Marie cycled back along the road that had brought her to Tailleville and would now take her home, she became aware that a motor vehicle was following her, its dimmed headlights visible from time to time in the distance. Unlike the vehicles she had encountered at the Kommandantur, whose panic-stricken drivers swore at her and almost ran her over, this vehicle was in no hurry. It crawled along at her own steady pace, always staying well back.

Instinct told her that its occupant was the Gestapo officer, Klemt. He was making sure she returned to Belville and did not try to escape from him. And now, just as she had been trapped at the Kommandantur and unable to flee from him, so she found herself cornered again. There was no way she could shake him off, and it was pointless to try hiding from him down a side road; he knew where to find her. She could only hope that her instinct was wrong and it was not him in the vehicle, or that he would lose interest or had some other reason to be on the road, and the headlights would turn away or vanish. But they stayed just where they were, as if joined to her by an invisible cord.

The patrols she had met earlier were gone. In Belville, nothing stirred. The moon was bright and the sky cloudless, but fingers of grey above the horizon promised that dawn was on the way. The villagers who had gathered in the lane earlier to watch the bombing of Caen had retreated indoors, either trying to resume their interrupted night's sleep or waiting anxiously to see what else the night might bring.

She returned her bicycle to its usual place beside the little greenhouse. She spent a minute or so in the greenhouse, then went to the front door just in time to hear the deep exhaust note of a vehicle arriving outside. She opened the door. There in the lane was the same black car that had brought Klemt here previously. But this time it was the Gestapo major himself at the wheel. There was no driver with him. No one to witness whatever was to happen now – meaning whatever Klemt intended to happen.

He cut the car's engine and there was silence. But it was not total silence. She could hear the whisper of the ocean, so familiar to her that it barely registered. But was there another sound beyond it tonight, or was that only her imagination? She stood there listening, her unwelcome visitor forgotten for the moment as she concentrated her attention on that sound that should not have been there.

Klemt stepped out of the car. He swayed unsteadily. 'What are you doing?'

She did not answer him. He stood beside her and listened. The sound was stronger now.

'Aircraft,' he said. 'But not bombers, so there is nothing to worry about, dear little Marie. We will be safe and comfortable here. This is not another bombing raid. These are fighter planes we can hear – Luftwaffe planes, therefore. The Luftwaffe is protecting us.' A belch escaped him. 'The Reich has the very best fighter planes and pilots in the world.'

He was impatient. He gestured for her to go indoors, as though the place was his rather than hers. She struck a match and set about lighting the lantern, but her mind remained on the aircraft. They sounded closer now, and there were many of them. Were they truly Luftwaffe? No, she did not believe so. Klemt was wrong. They were coming over the English Channel.

'Why are you here?' she asked him. 'Why did you follow me?'

'Follow you? No, Marie, I *escorted* you, to ensure your safety. You should not be alone on this dangerous night. I told you that.'

'Just now, you told me we'll be safe.'

'And we are. I will keep you safe.'

'You and the Luftwaffe?'

'Now you are trying to be clever. Tonight is a night when we should get to know one another. Let us be friends.'

'Friends?'

'Certainly. Why not? You were good friends with your Oberleutnant Hauser, so I am sure you can be friends with me.' He attempted a smile; it was a leer. 'I think you know the kind of friendship I have in mind. Pretty little Marie – you seem so innocent, but I think you know very well what men require – German men, men of the great German Reich. I think Oberleutnant Hauser would have taught you well, whatever his other failings. Tell me, where is the beautiful lingerie I saw on my last visit?'

He had brought a bottle of wine. He placed it on the table and she saw its label. It was one of the bottles he had accused Heinrich of stealing in order to sell on the black market.

A cold anger bloomed in her. Ever since she had noted those dimmed headlights following her on the road, she had been fearful. But now, at the sight of that bottle of wine, there was fury as well. This beast, this monster, who certainly needed no more to drink, was planning to gorge himself on the very wine with which he had cheated Heinrich of his freedom and possibly his life. Not content with that, he thought he could have what he wanted from her, cheating Heini of even his Marie. And he even wanted the lingerie Heini had given her to be part of his obscene pleasure.

She ignored his question. Instead, she went to the doorway and looked out. The aircraft had now come close enough to be visible in the moonlit sky, though they were still not identifiable; they seemed to be holding position over the coast.

'You're wrong about those aircraft,' she said, thinking to shake his complacency. 'They're not Luftwaffe. They've come from England.'

But he paid no heed. He was too busy with his sordid preparations, finding glasses for the wine and bringing them to the table. She shrugged. Why should she care if he was too stupid to be warned? He produced a corkscrew and opened the bottle, then removed his uniform tunic and his cap, clearly intent on taking his ease. His scalp beneath the cropped blonde hair was pink and somehow vulnerable, but vulnerable in the manner of a reptile hatchling, and just as revolting, a thing to be crushed underfoot. He stood close to her, too close, and stroked her cheek with his bony finger as he had done on the day he took Heinrich away. He lurched even closer, the thin lips attempting to kiss her. His breath was rancid. She turned her face away.

'That beautiful lingerie I saw,' he said. 'Why don't you fetch some of it?'

The aircraft were circling in tight formation. They were very high and beyond the reach of the anti-aircraft batteries, as though waiting in readiness for whatever their role was to be. Sirens were sounding, searchlight beams swept back and forth, bursts of flak peppered the sky. Why would German defences sound an alarm, search out and attack their own Luftwaffe fighters? So it was certain. All doubt had been removed: these aircraft were not Luftwaffe.

First the bombing of Caen. And now this.

But Klemt was oblivious to what was happening on the coast and to what she could see and hear. He was like an animal capable of only one thought, one primitive urge. He lunged forward and tried to grab her but missed his footing and stumbled against her.

'Get back!' She shouted right into his face and pushed him away with both hands. 'Leave me alone!'

'But Marie –'

'Leave me alone – get out of my home!'

He closed in on her again. 'Leave you alone? No, I do not think so, little Marie.' His mood had darkened; his voice was hard. 'I do not think you want that at all.' He was unbuckling his belt with its eagle and swastika motif, and coiling it about his fist. 'Go to the bedroom. That's where little whores like you belong. Go to the bed and show me what you did for your Oberleutnant.'

'I'll see you in hell first!'

He swung the belt at her but she stepped aside. She tried to push him away again, but he was stronger than he looked, skeletal creature that he was. He held his ground, seized her shoulder with his free hand and propelled her across the room towards the bedroom. She recovered her balance and turned back to face him. She had known it would come to this, had known that in the end there would be only one way to deal with this monster. She was ready for what she had to do now, had prepared herself for it when she went to the greenhouse.

Klemt's eyes grew wide as she lifted her blouse clear

of her skirt, raising it so high that she exposed not only her midriff but also the lower curve of her naked breasts.

'Is this what you want? Are these what you're after?'

His mouth fell open. But she was not finished; she had a further surprise for him.

'Or what about this?'

His eyes grew even wider when he saw the .38 revolver she drew from the waistband of the skirt. The only gift Archie had ever given her.

Klemt stared at the weapon. Then he burst out laughing.

'You would shoot me, Marie? This is your plan? Have you ever shot a man before? Have you even fired a gun? Look at you – you can hardly hold it steady to aim it!'

But she had no chance to shoot, and he had no chance to use the Luger he was struggling to free from its holster. A loud hissing filled the air, startling both of them. It was followed by the dull crump of an explosion, so close to the cottage that the walls shook. Then came another, this time a direct hit. The front of the cottage collapsed inward. The door frame bent and split, the door splintering into pieces. Klemt flung his arms up to protect himself as the timber beams and blocks of stone tumbled on top of him. He made no sound as he went down and was lost from view in a cloud of white dust.

'Marie! Marie!'

Simone was calling her. Marie heard her but could not see her, the dust obscuring everything. Then Simone seized her arm, and together they stumbled out of the rubble of the cottage. Shells continued to whistle past and explode. Simone took her all the way down to the far boundary of the yard, to a drainage ditch topped by dense hedging.

'This is the safest place,' she said. 'Don't go back to the cottage. Stay right here until the shelling stops or moves on to another sector. Don't go into the barn. Buildings are dangerous. Outdoors is safer – nothing to fall on you. Keep that pistol at the ready in case any retreating Boche pass through here and find you. They won't be feeling very friendly.'

'Why are we being shelled? Is this the invasion?'

'Yes, and we're on the front line – the landing beaches are here, in Normandy. London says there are hundreds of warships off the coast. Thousands of men are disembarking, fighting their way ashore. The shelling is to give them cover. No one is shooting at us deliberately, it's just that they're trying to get the range right. But it's happening, Marie, it really is. It's all over for the Boche, they're finished. My God, how we've waited!'

Shells continued to whistle and explode. From this angle, Marie could see the backs of Belville's other cottages. Her home was not the only one to be hit. But now, mercifully, the shells were beginning to fall short.

She turned her gaze towards the coast. It was a very different picture she saw now compared with earlier. Now she understood the purpose of the aircraft that had been circling. They had broken away from their holding pattern and were dispersed over a wide area. Some were attacking targets at ground level – surely all those bunkers and gun emplacements and radar stations of the Atlantic Wall – while others were engaged in aerial combat with German fighters, the Luftwaffe of which Klemt had boasted. The sky was alive with aircraft, weaving and climbing and diving in every direction, in what seemed like complete chaos. Bright flashes of gunfire criss-crossed the sky. The roar of anti-aircraft fire and explosions was distant but continuous. The coastline had become a battle zone.

'Get down, Marie,' Simone was insisting. 'Get down and stay down.'

Marie took a final glance at the patch of sky directly overhead, the only view she had from the depths of the ditch. Seagulls passed overhead, fleeing from the coast and complaining loudly. The moon was still visible but was being washed pale by the bright morning sunlight.

Dawn had arrived.

Heinrich slammed on the brakes. The Opel slewed across the narrow road and skidded to a halt.

Before him drifted a pall of smoke and dust. Shells were landing and exploding along Belville's lanes. Cottages that had escaped the accidental bombing last year had been less fortunate this time. Holes had been torn in their walls and roofs. Some were on fire. A number of villagers were pumping water to fill buckets and any other containers with which to fight the flames; others were digging through rubble to rescue family members or neighbours. He remembered the same task a year ago. He had been able to help the people of Belville then, he and his men. But he could not help them this time.

The smoke cleared enough for him to see Marie's cottage. The front wall was gone. The thatched roof looked ready to cave in. Timber beams and whitewashed stones from the shattered wall covered the floor among the remains of pieces of furniture. He could make out the table and two broken chairs, and the couch upended and crushed: once-familiar things from a faraway life he had once known. What a sweet life it had been. Now there was only destruction here.

In front of the cottage stood a black Mercedes sedan. It was covered in dust and dirt but showed no sign of any damage. He knew whose vehicle it was.

The lanes were littered with debris and shell fragments that the Opel would not be able to negotiate. He would have to go on foot from here. He climbed down from the truck, cursing his injuries that made every movement so slow. He headed for the cottage, limping through the debris and crouching low whenever he heard the whistle of an incoming shell. Such a short distance, but for him it was a marathon journey. A few of the villagers glanced at him but no one recognised him.

As he stopped to rest for a moment, he looked up, and there was Simone rounding the corner of the cottage. She stopped in her tracks and stared at him. He waited. Then recognition dawned in her eyes.

'Heinrich? My God, Heinrich, what have they done to you?'

'Where is she? Where is Marie?' He spoke slowly, knowing that his speech was unclear because of the damage to his jaw and mouth.

Simone nodded to show she understood not only his words but also his difficulty in enunciating them.

'She's here with me, Heinrich. She's fine, absolutely fine.'

'And Klemt? I know he's here somewhere. So where is he?'

'Herr Gestapo? See for yourself. He won't be troubling anyone ever again.'

He followed her gaze towards the ruined interior of the cottage. It was hard for him to focus. He went closer. In a gap between fallen stones, he made out first a jackbooted leg and then the rest of the body, coated in dust, lying face down. But there was enough of the cropped blonde hair and pink scalp still visible for him to know it was Klemt. A little further off were a uniform cap and a tunic, both of them half buried but undamaged. It was as though the Gestapo man had removed them voluntarily rather than that they had been torn off by the blast of an explosion. What had he been doing that led him to shed his clothing? Heinrich turned his good eye questioningly on Simone.

'It's all right,' she said, understanding what he was

asking. 'He did nothing to her. Nothing.'

'And the Engländer? Where is he?'

'He's gone.'

'By means of your network?'

'No. London sent an aircraft for him.'

'Did they indeed? No half measures, then.'

'They wanted him back urgently.'

Heinrich sighed. He was weary, so very weary, weary to his bones. He had been standing here for long enough, too long. His body ached, every part of it. He could feel his strength ebbing.

So the Engländer was gone.

Only one thing mattered now.

'Take me to Marie.'

'Of course.'

He took a look around, at the lane and the cottages. As suddenly as it had begun, the bombardment had ended.

He summoned the last of his strength and followed Simone into Marie's yard. It was a homecoming of sorts.

Marie climbed up from the ditch, gulping lungfuls of air as if she had been deprived of oxygen. There was movement near the cottage. Simone was returning. A man was with her – he was German, for he was draped in a Wehrmacht greatcoat. Perhaps he was one of the retreating Germans that Simone had warned her about. Perhaps Simone had taken him prisoner, for if this was indeed the invasion, then everything might be different now, the Germans no longer the masters and no need for Simone to remain under cover.

The greatcoat seemed to be too large for the man. And now Marie saw that Simone was not in fact holding him at gunpoint as she had supposed; he was not her prisoner. But if he was German and not a prisoner but at liberty, who was he and what was he doing here? Was it wise not to have him under armed guard? What was Simone thinking, she who was always so cautious?

Marie closed her hand on the revolver. Archie's revolver. She disengaged the safety.

The man was limping, hunched over, and seemed to be very old, his steps so slow and painful that Simone had to adjust her pace. He was nursing his right hand, which was misshapen and bent at an unnatural angle. As he came closer, Marie saw that his face was a mass of bruises, purple and distended. His nose was broken, for it was flat like a boxer's and twisted to one side. Only one eye, his right eye, peered at her from a narrow slit in that pulverised face; the left eye was lost beneath the bruises.

Simone brought him to within a few paces of Marie, as if that was his destination. But why? Marie did not know this man. She shuddered at the mere sight of him, so twisted and battered that he barely seemed human. A pathetic creature, a Quasimodo. Who was he and why was he here?

He stood there, staring at her with that terrible eye as though he expected something from her. He seemed to be struggling for breath.

'Meine Liebe,' he whispered hoarsely.

Heinrich saw the revulsion in Marie's face. It pierced him to the heart to see it, and for a moment his thoughts were all about himself, a deep sorrow that his beloved Marie should recoil from him in such a way, after everything he had been through, after all his suffering.

And now, suddenly, there was fear in her eyes as well.

'Don't be afraid,' he told her, his voice no more than a whisper.

But he understood, he knew the reason. It was only to be expected, he told himself. She did not recognise him, that was all, nothing more than that. It was not fear of *him*, not really, it was not revulsion from *him*; these emotions were simply her reaction to this wreck of a human being that had taken his place. As soon as she realised that this was truly her Heini and he had come back to her –

But his thoughts got no further. She had paid no heed to his whispered words. Or perhaps she had not heard, the whisper was so faint. But something was happening, something he did not understand. Once again, he cursed his infirmities. His field of vision was limited, and he did not see where the pistol, a revolver, had come from, but suddenly there it was, in Marie's hands. He found himself looking down the muzzle of the weapon as she raised it.

She opened fire.

Part Four
By Moonlight

Seb Wetherick was as good as his word. In the nights that followed the D-Day invasion, Archie and the other pilots of 161 Squadron had plenty to do – pick-ups and drops across France as the Allies pushed forward and the Germans tried to hold their lines. There were agents to deliver and some to bring out with crucial and time-sensitive intelligence for London: documents, maps, engineering drawings of newly developed German munitions – including, it was rumoured, Hitler's 'wonder weapons' – all of it physical material that had to be delivered by hand.

Archie did more than his share. Marie was never far from his thoughts, even his dreams, so he was grateful for his duties and the distraction they offered.

Then the day came when Seb had a very particular job for him.

'It's a pick-up. Urgent. You'll go tonight, weather permitting. The moon is still good. You'll be collecting one of our best agents, according to our friends in the Secret Intelligence Service. A spy who goes by the code name Virgil. That's all I've been told, that's all I'm allowed to know – the usual precautions. This Virgil has specifically asked to be brought out, and urgently. SIS always oblige when an agent makes a request to leave the field, especially an urgent one like this. They received the message only today, so as you can see, we're not hanging about. Virgil assures them that everything can be organised for a safe landing and exit tonight. Now, are you up for it, Archie?' Seb eased himself back in his chair with an ironic smile. 'Not got any prior engagements?'

Archie shook his head. 'No prior engagements.'

Seb puffed on his pipe and studied him for a moment.

'I think you'll enjoy this job. It's why I'm chalking it up to you.'

'I always enjoy them, Seb. So why do you say that?'

'Because you'll be going back to Normandy. Actually, to the precise same spot we collected you from. A little place called Belville, if I remember correctly. If I'm not mistaken. Have I got that right?'

Belville. Archie saw everything as clearly as it was that night: Marie's pasture, the flarepath, that lonely figure watching as he disappeared into the night sky.

Seb was waiting for a reply.

'When are you ever mistaken, Seb?'

The commander squinted into the bowl of his pipe. 'Not often, Archie. Not often.'

Archie went off to prepare his maps.

So Seb had seen the notes of his debrief in leafy Berkshire, the debrief that had never happened, its notes written by Mr Tyler and Miss Bryant who were never there.

But what was the secret that, according to Seb, Archie apparently knew but was not supposed to know, the secret he did not know he knew?

A silly riddle.

For a time, it seemed that the operation might be off. The weather through the evening was unsettled – blustery wind and rain, and cloud cover that obscured the moon. But by 2330 hours, the sky had cleared and an encouraging forecast promised a calm night over the English Channel and in Normandy, with no cloud. Archie seized his chance and was in the air by midnight.

He reached the Normandy coast without incident. But nothing could have prepared him for what he saw there. It was transformed tonight from the last time he had seen it. He had known theoretically what to expect, but the reality still left him in awe. Ships beyond number crowded the sea off the landing beaches, vessels of all sizes and types: destroyers, battleships, cruisers, cargo ships, frigates. He had never seen so many ships gathered together in one place. The landing craft were still there, abandoned now, having done their job. He saw the Mulberry harbours, the floating harbours that had been towed across the English Channel and would continue to be needed by Allied forces until enough French ports could be taken back from German control.

The land that lay ahead of him was different too. Tonight the monochrome panorama he was approaching was alive with vivid flares of explosions. They made the point that D-Day was a beginning, not an end. This was still a dangerous place. He knew that the anti-aircraft batteries had been knocked out of action, but he still had to watch out for German fighter aircraft.

He came in over the stretch of coast that he now knew was code-named Gold Beach. The Atlantic Wall had well and truly fallen here, had been ripped apart, but at a high cost in terms of casualties, and the evidence of the landings and the battle that had followed was everywhere: shattered concrete bunkers, chunks of shrapnel, the twisted metal of beach obstacles, abandoned equipment and weaponry, even bicycles that the Allied forces had brought with them, burnt-out tanks and other vehicles, a downed Luftwaffe fighter plane. He saw many dead bodies – far too many, regardless of which side they belonged to – on the sands, in the dunes, among the clumps of dune grass, in the lanes. In time they would be collected and buried respectfully, of whatever nation, German or Allies.

Further inland he saw pale shapes motionless in the

fields: farm animals killed by artillery fire. Man's wars devoured the innocent.

Two minutes later, there was the ruined church – the graveyard with its tombs, the ancient yew tree, the tower and spire. He remembered his despair on seeing the state of the church the day he arrived in Belville, remembered his first sight of Marie in her yard. And now here was her cottage; here was the yard with the water pump.

But the once neat and perfect little cottage was a ruin. Its front had been demolished, and the thatched roof hung above broken stones and debris spilling from the cottage and into the lane. He caught a glimpse of a bedroom, its wall gone, and of a bed complete with mattress half buried by the debris. His heart turned over. He knew that bed and its torn mattress.

He took in the rest of the village as he passed over it. Many other cottages that he remembered previously being more or less intact were now in ruins. The lanes were pitted with shell craters. Once again Belville had paid a high price for this war.

His heart was pounding. What had become of Marie?

He followed procedure: he circled the area to check for any signs of potential danger, then he looped around again. He had been heard and probably also seen, for a light flashed in Marie's pasture: dash–dash for M. It was the correct letter. Simone – if indeed it was Simone down there – had learned well. He replied: dash–dash–dot for G.

At once, the three lights of the flarepath came on, forming the familiar inverted L. Less than a minute later, he had landed safely and was in position ready for take-off.

Now came a familiar moment of nervousness as several figures – he counted half a dozen – emerged from

232

the ruins of the church, silhouettes armed with submachine guns. They halted at the edge of the pasture. If there were any surviving Germans in the area, if they had overpowered Archie's reception committee, obtained the recognition code and organised an ambush, then here they were now, and this was their time; the advantage was wholly theirs. Faced by so many of them, he would be in serious trouble. In his hand was a semi-automatic pistol. Better than his faithful old .38 but a totally inadequate defence against those submachine guns if this was an ambush.

He unlocked the cockpit roof and slid it open, and did what he had never done before on foreign soil: he shut the Lysander's engine down, freed himself from his harness, climbed out of the cockpit and swung down to the ground. He was putting himself at the point of maximum danger. Definitely not textbook.

One of the figures separated itself from the others and approached him. A tall, slim female figure, its shoulders made broad by a man's suit jacket. It was Simone. He breathed more easily. There was no ambush, but he recalled their last encounter, the bitter accusation he had made, and the vicious slap she had dealt him in response. She too would be remembering that moment.

'So they've sent you, Archie.' She glanced down at the pistol. 'Relax, you're among friends, and the Boche are gone – well, they're gone from this area, at least.'

He was aware of the steady rattle of gunfire in the distance somewhere inland – the far distance, thankfully. He put the pistol away.

'I assume it was you who sent the message to London on behalf of Virgil?'

She nodded. 'I'm Virgil's communication link. I

233

always have been. Virgil is –'

He cut across her. He did not care about Virgil. Not right now. He had been sent here for Virgil, but it was not for Virgil that he had climbed down from the Lysander.

'Is Marie here? Is she all right? Her cottage –'

It was his turn to be interrupted. Simone held up a hand to silence him.

'Patience, Archie.'

She was no longer looking at him. He turned to see what had taken her attention. The figures that had emerged with her from the church had not moved, but two others had now appeared and were approaching across the pasture, moving slowly from the darkness into the moonlight.

His heart soared. One of them was Marie. There was no mistaking that slight figure. But why was she moving so slowly, as if in pain?

'Something's wrong, Simone. Marie is injured.'

Simone shook her head.

He looked again. And this time saw that the difficulty was not with Marie but with the man who was her companion. His body was bent and stooped, and he was leaning heavily on her for support as he limped across the grassy pasture.

'Listen to me, Archie,' Simone was saying. 'I remind you, you're here for Virgil. He has a request to make, an important request. It has my full support.' She turned to look directly at Archie. 'Affairs of the heart are not our business tonight. Our sole concern is Virgil's request. Remember that.'

At last the pair reached the Lysander. Archie could not take his eyes off Marie, but Marie's gaze remained on her companion, on Virgil.

It was Virgil who spoke. He was barely audible. Archie strained to hear him.

'It's good to see you again, Engländer.'

That voice . . .

Archie stared at the man. He recognised that voice, even though the words it spoke were mumbled and unclear, as if the man's mouth was damaged. Which it most likely was, for in fact his entire face was a confusion of discoloured bruises. One eye peered at Archie; the other was a closed slit. Archie stared back at the battered face, at the bruises and crushed nose, and at that disconcerting solitary eye that was studying him. In the end, the voice, weak and distorted as it was, was more recognisable than the face.

'Heinrich?'

He had never addressed the German by name before. He thought of Mr Tyler and Miss Bryant and their mulish questions.

The German nodded wearily, as though the fact of his identity was surely obvious.

So this was the secret that SIS were guarding so jealously, the ultimate secret of Belville. 'One of our best agents,' according to the spymasters. This was the answer to the riddle, the secret that Archie knew but did not know he knew. Heinrich himself was that secret.

And now, like a man returned from the dead, here he was. God alone knew what he had suffered at the hands of the Gestapo, though some of the evidence was plain enough in that face and damaged body. God alone knew how he had escaped. During his time in Gestapo custody, had he been as strong as Marie had insisted to Archie he would be?

But all of that would be for SIS to establish; it would

be their problem. Archie had a different concern: what did the German's return mean for Marie? Now he understood Simone's warning about matters of the heart.

Heinrich spoke again, slowly and carefully.

'I need your help, Engländer. It is a simple thing I ask. I want you to take Marie to England tonight instead of me. Very soon now, France will become too dangerous for her. Do you understand why?'

'Because of her association with you. Your relationship.'

Heinrich nodded. 'I admit my error. It was a risk I never intended, a risk for Marie.' He turned his head so that his good eye was looking at her. 'Ach, we all make mistakes when we're in love, don't we, meine Liebe?'

She returned Heinrich's gaze but did not speak or react.

Simone took over from Heinrich. 'When France is liberated, there'll be purges, a hunt for collaborators. People will want blood. It will be just as I once told you, Archie. It will be a time when judgements will be made – who was a friend, who was a foe, who was a traitor? Unfortunately, not all judgements will be made correctly. People will tear each other apart. Often, the most vicious will be those who themselves have something to hide, some act or behaviour they're ashamed of – they'll want to deflect attention from themselves. There'll be accusations, public humiliation, retribution, even summary executions. These things will happen, be sure of that. They happened after the last war, the Great War, and they'll happen again, and the innocent will be swept away with the guilty. This is the danger for Marie. We must get her away from Belville – she has to leave France. It's the only way for her protection.'

Still Marie said nothing.

Archie returned his attention to Heinrich. 'What are your plans now?'

Heinrich shrugged. 'For me, nothing changes. I will continue my work here in France. You can assure London of that. The forces of the Reich are in retreat, but their defeat will take many months yet. I am confident my cover is intact. The man who arrested me is dead. The case against me, such as it was, dies with him. I doubt if there is even a formal record of it – and if there is, it will be lost or forgotten in the confusion that lies ahead. Thanks to that same confusion it will be possible for me to resume my position as a Wehrmacht officer. In its dying days, the Reich will welcome all the manpower it can get.'

'Why did you tell London you wanted to leave the field? Why not simply make an official request for Marie to be taken to England?'

Heinrich was reaching the end of his strength. Each time his eye blinked, it remained closed for a second or two.

'Make my apologies to London for my small subterfuge. Official requests of that sort take time – time we may not have. Also too dangerous – there would be paperwork that could fall into the wrong hands and lead back to me. Marie risked her life for both you and me, Engländer. Tonight you are in the privileged position of being able to repay that debt – if you are willing. Take her in that aircraft of yours, just as you had that advantage when London fetched you back. Your heart isn't stone. Will you do this?' He paused, wheezing. 'I ask as one soldier to another.'

Archie recognised the reference. But Heinrich had no need to call in favours. The textbook rule that Archie as pilot had total authority still stood – but tonight he extended it to take account of the views of one other person. The most important person of all.

'I'll take Marie to England.' He was replying to Heinrich but he was looking at Marie because his words were for her. 'Provided that's what she wants.'

Heinrich nodded in agreement. 'Of course.' He placed his hand gently on Marie's arm. 'Meine Liebe, what do you want to do? Will you go to England?'

She looked from Heinrich to Simone, then to Archie, and at last he understood her silence tonight, her reticence, watching and listening but saying nothing, letting the scene play out while she kept her own counsel. She had come to tonight's encounter aware of the decision she had to make, the most momentous decision of her life: whether or not to leave France, with the very real possibility that she would never be able to return. Heinrich and Simone had shielded and protected her up to now, but they had also shaped her life and her world, confident that they always knew what was best for her – even if that happened to suit them too. But no more. Archie sensed that something had changed since he was last here. The bonds between them were still strong, but a balance of some kind had shifted. He was certain of that, though he did not know what had caused it. But it meant that Marie would make her decision on her own. Not with Heinrich, not with Simone, but on her own. Just as he had always said she was capable of doing.

And now it was time for that decision.

A few minutes later, Heinrich stood alone in the pasture. Simone and her comrades had melted into the night. The sound of the departing Lysander faded to nothing, and he was left with only the lonely sigh of the ocean.

He had lost Marie, his sweet Marie. He felt no bitterness, no rancour. All he had ever wanted was to know she was safe; this was all he had hoped for as he raced back to Belville on his escape from Caen. In the days since then, days when she had nursed him as once she had nursed the young Engländer, he had never asked her about the Engländer and what her feelings were for him. He respected the secrets of her heart. They should remain exactly that: secrets.

'Ach, so many secrets! We live by secrets!'

He lit a cigarette and waited until he felt strong enough to walk unassisted. There was no Marie to support him; there never would be now. As he made his way slowly towards the graveyard, he thought about the people of Belville. In what remained of their ruined homes, behind their closed doors and shuttered windows, they too would be listening to the night, waiting patiently for an end to war. And watching him, no doubt.

They had always known he had his secrets. It was an imprecise awareness: they had no knowledge of what those secrets might be, only an instinctive understanding, like their religious faith. And like that faith, it was something they did not question, something that did not require investigation or discussion. Along with Simone and her comrades, they had protected him well and kept his secrets – just as they also protected Simone and her men. Now he would look to the people of Belville for continued protection while his body healed sufficiently for him to pursue his plans. He was strong; the healing would not take too long.

He took the keys from his pocket and unlocked the bronze door of the tomb. He had brought one of the flashlights from the pasture. He spent some time checking the contents of the tomb. The goods he had concealed from Klemt were much as he had left them – correction: much as he and the Engländer had left them – and they would continue to be safe here.

He would not be returning to the Kommandantur in Tailleville. It would be abandoned, seized by the advancing Allied forces, all its files and records deliberately destroyed in the general rout and retreat – which would suit his purpose perfectly. So would the fact that Klemt was dead. As the giant corporal had said, dead men told no tales. When he was up to the task, he would find a way to cross the battle lines and join another Wehrmacht unit, just as he had told the Engländer he would. It could be done: in the confusion of war, the lines could be crossed if a man knew what he was doing and was careful. He would keep his word and resume his intelligence work.

But he would do more than that – for there would be good business to be transacted as well as intelligence to be gathered. Retreating armies looted and destroyed, discipline broke down, chaos took command. No better time to acquire goods, no better time to deal and trade. He would barter, converting as much as he could into portable assets – gold or diamonds. He had the contacts for that. When the fighting finally ended, he would be ready. He might not measure up to what the corporal had said of Klemt, he might not become one of Germany's richest men, but he would have enough – more than enough, more than a boy from the back alleys of Berlin would ever have thought possible. When a new world began to rise from the ashes of the old, he would place his investments: the construction industry or perhaps engineering or manufacturing. There would be wealth to be gained, fortunes to be won in that new world if a man seized the right opportunities.

Heinrich Hauser would be that man. He would seize those opportunities. In that new world, no possibility would be beyond his reach.

And eventually, like the rest of his body, his heart would heal.

Marie watched as Archie's aircraft climbed into the night sky, a fleeting silhouette against the moon. She pictured the rippling ocean over which the aircraft would pass, and wondered how it must feel to be up there among the stars and see the whole world from horizon to horizon.

She remembered that pale dawn when thousands of Allied soldiers had fought their way from that ocean and over the beaches of Normandy, when the sky swarmed with aircraft and the Atlantic Wall was torn apart.

She remembered her horror at the sight of the man that Simone had brought to her that morning.

'Meine Liebe,' he had whispered.

The words had struck her like a thunderbolt. But she had drawn back from him in revulsion, turned her gaze away. This Quasimodo, this malformed remnant of a man, this was surely not her Heinrich.

But it was. It was Heini. By some miracle, he had come back to Belville. What hell he had been through and what dangers he had survived, she could not imagine. But he had done it, he had survived.

Before she could say anything in reply to him, before she could try to make amends for her first reaction, a movement behind him caught her attention. Something or someone was moving in the ruins of her cottage. The quiver of movement came again, and she knew she was not mistaken.

A figure stepped clear from the rubble, a figure caked from head to foot in white dust. It was Klemt, the monster who was supposed to be dead. His arm was outstretched and he was holding the Luger he had been too drunk to use earlier, too drunk even to free it from its holster. But she was certain he was not drunk now, and the weapon was aimed at the three of them, at herself,

Heinrich and Simone.

Only she had seen him, only she was facing in that direction. There was no time for her to warn the others, no time even to think; there was time only for her to act. She still held Archie's revolver, loaded and ready. In one instinctive move, with no pause to take aim and hidden from Klemt's view by Heinrich, she gripped the revolver in both hands, raised her arms, and fired – and saw the ghost-like figure stumble backwards with the impact and then fall to the ground. She knew that this time it would not rise up again.

Simone seemed rooted to the spot as if unable to take in what had happened, unable to believe what Marie had just done. Marie of all people. Marie who was little more than a child.

Heinrich had no such difficulty.

'You saved us, meine Liebe,' he whispered to Marie. 'You saved all of us.'

But tonight she knew that what she had done that morning was not enough. Eliminating one German, even a monster like Klemt, was not enough. And saving only Simone and Heinrich and herself, that too would never be enough. It was France that had to be saved. France itself. Nothing less.

'Meine Liebe, what do you want to do?' Heinrich had asked her as Archie and his aircraft waited. 'Will you go to England?'

Explosions thumped in the distance. She heard the rattle of machine-gun fire. The fighting inland was continuing. She looked around at her pasture, saw the ruins of her little cottage, the only home she had ever known, and the graveyard that was her mother and father's final resting place.

She knew what her decision had to be. It was the only decision possible. This was her France, and this was where she should be. Here and nowhere else. Not up there among the stars with Archie. And not in England with its fairy tales and kings and queens.

She lifted Heinrich's hand gently from her arm and kissed his ravaged cheek. She kissed Archie. She had a smile for him.

'Always so serious, Archie!'

Then she took her place at Simone's side.

'I'll fight for France,' she said. 'I'll stay in France and I'll fight for France.'

It was a perfect moon night. The Channel was calm, the moon unclouded and bright, and there was no sign of any impending change in the weather. No sign either of any Luftwaffe night fighters, but Archie continued to scan the horizon, the sky above him and the sea below, his eyes never resting. It was second nature to him.

Marie had once said that God had been kind to him. He had not contradicted her, but nor had he agreed with her. She had said he had been lucky. Well, he was a wiser man now, and he agreed with her now, whether it was God's kindness or blind luck: the ambush he had escaped from unscathed while poor Loïc Boiteux had died; his crash-landing; the perilous overland journey that had brought him to Belville; the fact that he had found a guardian in Heinrich – the most unexpected guardian imaginable.

Then there was his return to Belville tonight. The relief of finding Marie unharmed.

And he had discovered what it was to fall in love. True, he had also discovered the pain of love, but surely that was better than never loving at all. Some popular song or other, or some poet, must have said something along those lines.

One day, this war would end. He would return to France, to Belville. He would find Marie again. That would be the time for him to do what he had never dared to do, the time to take her in his arms and at last confess his love for her.

Perhaps by moonlight.

About the Author

I grew up in Northern Ireland with its breathtaking rural landscapes and coastal scenery. When we're young, we take so much for granted. The beauty of Northern Ireland, and my part of County Antrim in particular, is unsurpassed – yet to me it all seemed quite normal at the time.

In contrast, my university years were spent in Belfast during the violence of the Troubles. I discovered what it was like to live in a divided community – and one in which the military presence was overwhelming. There really was constant danger. You took care what streets you walked through, what bars you went to, what conversations you had with strangers, you watched what vehicles were approaching. I'm sure all of this must have influenced my writing – its themes and ideas but also the physical settings and their emotional impact.

After a career in advertising and marketing, I now write full-time. I am a Gold winner in the prestigious Foreword Indies Book of the Year awards. *Spies by Moonlight* is my sixth novel.

www.kevindoherty.com

www.blossomspringpublishing.com

Printed in Dunstable, United Kingdom

66776368R00150